LIPS OF AN ANGEL

A RIVER WINERY NOVEL

JEN TALTY

of the romance grabs you emotionally and the suspense keeps you sitting on the edge of your chair. Great characters, great writing, and a believable plot that can be a warning to all of us." *Desiree Holt, USA Today Bestseller*

"*Dark Water* delivers an engaging portrait of wounded hearts as the memorable characters take you on a healing journey of love. A mysterious death brings danger and intrigue into the drama, while sultry passions brew into a believable plot that melts the reader's heart. Jen Talty pens an entertaining romance that grips the heart as the colorful and dangerous story unfolds into a chilling ending." *Night Owl Reviews*

"This is not the typical love story, nor is it the typical mystery. The characters are well rounded and interesting." *You Gotta Read Reviews*

"*Murder in Paradise Bay* is a fast-paced romantic thriller with plenty of twists and turns to keep you guessing until the end. You won't want to miss this one..." *USA Today bestselling author Janice Maynard*

BOOK DESCRIPTION

She was only supposed to help with his son...only she showed him what family and love was truly about.

Toby Tillman was done. He'd put up with his soon-to-be ex-wife's shenanigans for long enough. It was time to take matters into his own hands. He'd do whatever it took to ensure TJ grew up in a loving environment, with a father who put him first.

He wasn't prepared, however, for Zinfandel River - all grown up and ready to take on the world. Not only was she willing to put herself in the line of fire, but she was also ready to take on a troubled teenager - all while walking away with Toby's heart.

HAVE WE GOT A STORY FOR YOU!

Dear Readers:

Welcome to Candlewood Falls!

Each Candlewood Falls story stands alone. However, the end of one story doesn't mean the end of your favorite characters. They can show up in any Candlewood Falls book at any time.

Candlewood Falls is a unique world of connected stories by different authors whose characters, business, and events appear in each others' stories.

Think of Candlewood Falls as a literary soap opera.

Be sure to check out the the other authors and discover which other books include your favorite characters.

Happy reading!

Stacey Wilk & K.M Fawcett & Jen Talty

1

———

TOBY

oby Tillman couldn't take his eyes off Zinfandel River. His hand rested on the small of her back as they strolled down the path to her home.

The cottage on The River Winery property.

This was dangerous territory, considering he'd left once already when he took his son to his friend's house.

He tried not to think about what her family might think as he stared at her.

She had to be the most beautiful woman he'd ever laid eyes on with her long red hair and green eyes.

Stunning.

He'd always thought she'd been a cute kid when she babysat his son, full of energy and promise. Always rattling off something she'd learned in school. It drove his soon-to-be ex-wife crazy, and if he were being honest with himself, it kind of made him a little nuts too. He always thought she was too much like her mother, Weezer.

High-strung. A little left of normal.

Zinny beat to the tune of her own drummer. She once told him that life wasn't meant to be cookie-cutter. It was meant to be ridden like a bull. Wild and crazy. And if you didn't get tossed off so you could brush yourself off and get back on again, then you weren't doing life right.

He'd spent most of his youth trying to either get out of someone's shadow, trying to please other people, or doing his darndest not to be seen. By the time he was an adult and he'd married Serena, life had become about what others thought. What everyone else saw. Conversations at the dinner table with Serena focused on what she believed other people's perceptions were and how to make sure her family was seen in the correct light.

Zinny was proud to take on her mother's philosophy of *who gives a fuck* every day of the week. Zinny was proud of who she was and where she came from. If people didn't like her, she believed that was their loss. Her confidence was often contagious.

He'd always admired her ability to be a kid, and yet she had an old soul and always had a sense of maturity. Lately, all he saw was the woman. The smart, intelligent adult that for the last six months had been his rock. His sounding board.

His best friend.

He'd be lost without her and he wasn't quite sure where to file that.

He was sixteen years older, and he'd known her for her entire life. That alone should make him pause the insane thoughts swirling about his head. He wanted to pull her into his arms and kiss her until she begged him to stop.

Her family had invited him and his son TJ over for their weekly Sunday family dinner, and he wondered if anyone noticed how he couldn't stop staring. The River family had never been his biggest fan, and with good reason. Most people in Candlewood Falls remembered him for his antics when he played hockey, and his marriage to Serena with the way she treated everyone in town didn't help his reputation. He didn't blame anyone for the way they felt about him, especially now. But he had a son to protect, and after what his soon-to-be ex-wife had done, he was grateful that Carter, Zinfandel's father, had even agreed to be his lawyer in his divorce and custody hearing.

It shouldn't be a difficult case, considering his wife was awaiting trial for tampering with medical records, but that wasn't even the point. His son had been used as a pawn.

And he'd allowed it to happen.

He'd been complacent.

He'd been jealous and it was time to make some major changes.

"I hope everyone in my family was kind to you,"

Zinfandel said as she stood at her front door. Her long red hair flowed over her shoulders. Her sweet lips turned into a soft smile. Her green eyes caught the moonlight and lit up like an emerald.

The more time he spent with her, the more he knew he was falling head over heels. But there were so many reasons this was a bad idea.

He had a teenage son.

Depending on what happened with the trial, custody could be an all-out war.

He was much older.

And her mother was the Weezer.

"I took a few jabs here and there, but they were great. And they were even better to TJ. That's all I care about."

"He's such a great kid," she said. "Are you going to be okay with him spending the night at his friend's house? You looked kind of hurt that he didn't want to go home with you."

Toby chuckled. "I'm just glad his new teammates are accepting him and Dax is helping to make that happen."

"You and Dax friends." Zinny took some of her long hair into her fingers and shook her head. "I'm sure my sister never thought she'd see that day coming."

If he didn't leave soon, he might do something he couldn't undo. "Neither did I, but we all have to grow up sometime. It just took me longer than most." Toby licked his lips. He imagined she tasted like strawberries, considering she was always drinking that signature drink from the Green Bean.

He wanted to kiss her so bad, but there were so many reasons he shouldn't.

Their age difference for one.

The custody battle for two.

Her mother and her shotgun for three.

He cracked a smile on that thought. He'd seen firsthand Weezer go running down the street in a robe, curlers, and carrying that weapon all while chasing after Riesling's ex. It had been hilarious, and not just because it wasn't Toby being chased. He might not have been well liked, but Theo was despised.

And for good reason.

Weezer was a bear when it came to her family and that was something Toby could respect.

"Something has you amused," Zinfandel said as she twisted her hair. She didn't do that unless she was nervous about something.

That made his heart beat a little faster.

He felt like a stupid teenager out on a first date. But this was Zinfandel. Or Zinny as some of her family and friends called her and he'd known her forever. He shouldn't feel strange or awkward. She'd been his kid's babysitter and she'd been a good friend to him during the worst year of his life.

This was no big deal.

"I should probably go," he said regretfully. "Please

thank your family again for including me in their family picnic. I had an amazing time."

"I'm glad you and TJ could make it," she replied. "But I'm not ready for the night to end. Would you like to come in for a drink? I've got lots of wine, and not just Zinfandel. I've got all my siblings as well."

He tossed his head back and busted out in a belly laugh. "You know, I'm more of a Cab guy."

"I've got that too." She turned and punched a few numbers on the keypad. "Malbec and Merlot are working on creating a new wine line. I swear if Malbec has a girl, they will be naming that child Cabernet."

"Well, that will be sticking with the theme."

"Riesling didn't do that when she had her kid."

"I believe she was being defiant." Toby stepped into the cabin. He'd never seen the inside of it before and he found it to be quaint.

But a little too intimate.

The bedroom, kitchen, and family room were all one space.

It didn't give him any way to detach all the inappropriate thoughts he was having as he stared at the bed, which had a crisp white comforter with navy-blue pillows and a couple of nautical throw pillows. He wanted to take them and toss them to the floor and pull back the sheets, climbing between them naked.

He inwardly groaned, tearing his eyes from the bed and focusing on the hard, uncomfortable-looking stool in the kitchen.

"How long have you lived here?" he asked, even though he knew the answer.

She tilted her head. "Seriously? You made fun of me for moving home," she said. "Remember, I was living in the townhouses on the edge of town for the last four years, but now that I'm learning more about the business, splitting my time between two jobs, this makes the most sense."

The one thing that could always be said about the River kids was that Carter and Weezer taught them how to be independent, even though they could all go back and work for the family business.

If they wanted.

Currently, Zinfandel worked for a company that sold the wine and had plans to work at the River Winery in the next five years. But she liked her independence.

Toby couldn't blame her.

"Yes. I knew that," he said. "I can't figure this one out though. Is everyone going to be working for the family business again?"

"Riesling never will. All my older brothers and sisters paved the way for me and the twins to work outside the winery. I think that's been good for us. It's given us a different perspective that we can bring back to the winery and that can only help. I feel like if it weren't for Malbec and his feud with my mom, we would have all been cogs in the machine. Now we have choices, and my mom is happy to bring us back into the fold."

"I remember when Malbec left. You were what, three years old?" Toby's mind struggled between what he wanted and trying to talk himself out of following through. Maybe if he focused on family history, he'd be able to keep his hands to himself.

"If that." She pulled down a bottle of wine from an impressive collection and uncorked it, pouring two glasses. She handed him one. "Why don't we sit in the family room."

He turned and chuckled. "Because that room is so far away." He took a seat on the sofa, where she joined him, tucking her feet up under her adorable ass.

The only problem was that he stared at her bed.

And that put thoughts in his brain again.

Not that he needed any help with that. Just staring into her intense green eyes gave him ideas. He wasn't quite sure when the shift from seeing her as a sexy, desirable woman had happened. It was like one day she was a kid and the next day an adult.

For months now he'd been fighting this feeling. Every time she'd shown up to help with TJ, he'd have to look the other way. Avoid catching her gaze. He'd been awkward and clunky around her and it drove him crazy. He worried people noticed.

Especially her father, Carter. Tonight he kept giving him the evil stink eye. Toby had become more terrified of him than Weezer, which never happened.

Worst part about that was he had an appointment

with Carter in two weeks to discuss his divorce. And full custody of his son. That was most important.

"I might have been a baby when my oldest brother left, but I remember how it affected my family. My siblings, especially Chablis. But mostly because she didn't come home very often. I missed her a lot."

"She was away at college?" Toby hadn't been tight with any of the River children. Not even when he and Dax were on the same hockey teams and Dax was dating Chablis.

But that was because Toby was an asshole back then, something he had no intention of ever becoming again.

"She had just graduated. Merlot was in college and Riesling was doing her own thing as well. Basically, my twin brothers and I might as well have been raised by two different sets of parents."

"Okay. I have to ask. When did your parents get divorced? And are they getting remarried?"

"My dad moved out shortly after Riesling was born, so I've never lived with him with the exception of a few months right after college. But who knows if they will ever remarry. We're all waiting for my mother to kick him out or for Dad to leave. Them living together is weird. Having sleepovers is great. But constantly under the same roof, I don't know."

"No offense, but that had to have been a strange childhood." He leaned back, resting one hand over the back of the sofa, his hand dangerously close to her hair.

Her bare shoulder.

His fingers itched to touch her silky skin.

"No," she said. "But I think it's weird for everyone else in this town. However, for me and my family, it's just another day in the life with the Weezer."

God. Toby loved everything about Zinny's attitude. She had a breezy way about her and it was infectious. Not much ruffled her feathers, and if they did, she ruffled them right back.

"I'm probably going to get slapped, but you know you're a little bit like your mother."

Zinny raised her glass and took a large gulp. "Story of my life, but truthfully, being told that doesn't bother me. My mom is so misunderstood, it's sad. She behaves the way she does to keep most people at arm's length because she's really quite sensitive."

"After spending time with her today, I can see that." He found everyone in Zinny's family to be kind. Generous. And absolutely sensitive to his and his son's situation. They certainly didn't judge him for his bad decisions over the years. No. They treated him with respect.

Even Chablis and Dax, who had every right to hate him.

Toby set his drink on the coffee table and leaned closer. "Only, both of your parents, while they were nice to me, didn't like the way I kept eyeing you." Shit. What the hell was he doing with his lips so close to Zinny's? This was a mistake.

Forget the age difference.

She was his lawyer's daughter.

Fuck. She was Weezer's kid. That alone should scare the crap out of him.

But all he could think about was the fact his lips were about half an inch from hers and she'd rested her hands on his shoulders.

Her pink tongue peeked out and he caught it with his, sucking it into his mouth and turning what should have been an awkward moment where he pulled back and cleared his throat into a wet, hot, passionate kiss.

He wrapped his arms around her warm body. She had curves where a woman should. She was soft and sweet, and her lips were like an angel sent from heaven to remind him he was alive.

For years he'd been dead inside. His wife, Serena—

Toby broke off the kiss. "I can't do this." He held Zinfandel by the shoulders. He sucked in a harsh breath. It burned his lungs.

"Why not?" Her long reddish-brown eyelashes fluttered wildly over her green eyes.

"Zinny, I'm married."

"You're legally separated, and your divorce will be final in days." She waggled her finger in front of his face. "Not many people are allowed to call me that, but since I want more of what just happened, I'll let you."

"That can't happen again."

"That would be too bad because it was seriously a good kiss." She leaned over, pressing her breasts on his forearm as she snagged her glass of wine. It was a cumbrous reach, which meant she did it on purpose.

He smiled.

He shouldn't have, but he did.

Then he remembered all the reasons this couldn't ever be. "You used to babysit for TJ when you were a kid. Hell, you're barely an adult."

She jerked her head back and glared. "Did you seriously just say that to me?"

"Let's face it; I was sixteen, almost seventeen when you were born."

"Your point?" She arched a brow and sipped her wine.

"You are closer to my son's age than to my age."

She stood and strolled to the other side of the room, which took all of five steps. She ran her hand over the corner of her bed and smiled. "I see what's going on here."

"You do?" He swallowed his breath.

"Yeah. You're just too scared to have sex with me."

He coughed. He pounded the center of his chest and gasped for air. He found his beverage and tossed it back in three gulps. Wine wasn't meant to be drank that fast, but he didn't care. He needed a bit of courage to respond to her brashness.

She'd always been bold and had the ability to speak her mind.

No one could ever describe Zinfandel River as being shy.

"I don't think that's my problem."

"Tell me something." She plopped down on the mattress, scooting backward, leaning against the pillows, stretching out her legs, and crossing her ankles.

He groaned. Lifting his glass, he peered inside.

It was empty. He got up and went for the bottle, making sure he gave himself a healthy pour.

He was going to need it.

"What do you want to know?" Talking was good. Having a conversation meant his lips were moving against air.

Not against her body.

"How old were you when you lost your virginity?" she asked. "And be honest."

He downed more wine. That was an interesting question. "Why do you want to know?"

"I'm trying to prove a point."

"Seventeen. And for the record, I've only been with three women. I've been faithful to my wife our entire marriage, but we broke up when I was in college and I dated two other girls."

"So, Serena was your first?"

"She was. Did you want to know the details?"

Zinny raised her hand and scrunched her face. "God, no."

"Your turn, since we're playing this game." He couldn't believe he'd asked the question. It wasn't because he thought it was immature or anything.

Because he didn't. But he wasn't sure he wanted to know anything about her past sex life.

The idea that any man touched her made his blood boil with jealousy.

He hadn't even felt that way when he'd learned Serena had been cheating on him with TJ's biological father. He and Serena had been over for a long time. His only regret was that he hadn't seen what Serena had been planning on doing to Chablis and Dax.

He still felt horrible that Chablis' private life had been made so public.

"I was a little older. Nineteen."

"So, in college?"

She nodded. "But you're making me feel like a bit of a slut since I've had more—how do we say this— partners?"

He chuckled. "How many?"

"Five. I hate to admit that one was a one-night stand. I was twenty-two and on a—"

He held up his glass. "I don't want to know." He took a sip. "I can't decide if it will make me jealous or angry."

"Angry?"

"You're a special girl. You deserve the world. I'd hate for you to be used like that."

"And if I was the one doing the using?" She tilted her head and winked.

His body went into hyperdrive. He took a slow draw of his wine as he stared her down, refusing to break eye contact. Even if he tried, he wouldn't be able to. He was mesmerized by her stare. She held him captive and he stopped fighting.

His feet were cemented to the ground.

Or maybe he just didn't want to lift them past making it to the side of the bed. He stood next to the edge. His heart rate was out of control. He couldn't hear his own thoughts anymore, and he wasn't sure if that was a good thing or a bad thing because half his thoughts were about taking her to bed.

The other half were all the reasons he shouldn't.

She took his glass, setting it on the nightstand.

"I might be younger than you, but I'm not a child." She rose to her knees, resting her hands on his shoulders. "For months you've relied on me. Trusted me. Even flirted with me. Why are you all of a sudden backpedaling?"

He curled his fingers around her wrists with the intention of pushing her away, but instead, he ran his hands up and down her arms and continued to stare into those damn inviting eyes. They were welcoming orbs of desire. He'd be blind if he didn't see that.

The connection between them had grown and it was more than her willingness to be there for TJ.

She'd been there for him. She'd been a shoulder to lean on when his deepest, darkest fears about TJ's biological father materialized.

And she was right. She wasn't a kid. She was a grown woman who knew what she wanted. She'd made that clear to everyone. She wasn't afraid to speak her mind. She took life by the horns and went for it.

He admired that.

Sometimes he wished he could be more like Zinny.

"I don't know," he whispered. "I don't want to hurt you." He climbed onto the bed, pulling her close to his chest, holding her as tight as he could.

Her chest heaved up and down with every hot breath. "Why are you afraid that you will?"

"I have a fourteen-year-old son. He's my world. He's more important to me than anything and he will always come first. No matter what."

"I know that." She palmed his cheek. "I don't expect you to put me before him. I only ask that if we get naked between these sheets, you don't get naked with anyone else unless you tell me to take a hike."

He took her hand and kissed it. He'd never met anyone as honest as Zinny. She didn't mince her words; that was for sure.

"I'm a one-woman kind of man." That had always been true about Toby. He might have been a selfish prick when it came to playing hockey and he hadn't treated his teammates well, especially Dax during his teenaged years. But when it came to the ladies in his life, he'd never strayed.

Not even when things got really bad with Serena.

He'd made a commitment to her and TJ. Until Serena had stepped out on their marriage and then committed a crime by stealing medical records to make

Dax and Chablis look bad, Toby had been a dedicated family man.

Well, he was still devoted to his boy.

He took Zinny's chin with this thumb and forefinger, brushing his lips tenderly across her mouth, savoring her sugary taste. Everything about her had a burst of energy that couldn't be subdued.

His need to feel her skin against his got the better of him and he grappled with their clothing, tossing it from the bed like it was on fire.

She was soft, and her curves filled his hands perfectly. He kissed her neck. Her shoulders. And the center of her chest. She was like one of those flowers that looked delicate from a distance, but when you got up close and personal, you realized there was nothing delicate about it.

It was strong and solid and so much more than something pretty to look at.

He cupped the swell of her breast with one hand while taking the puckered nipple of the other between his teeth.

She arched, groaning.

Every muscle exploded with excitement. It was as if he were sitting at the top of a roller coaster, in the front seat, teetering on the edge, waiting for the ride to begin. All the adrenaline rushing to every part of his body.

He continued to make his way down her stomach. Her belly was flat, but not too muscular.

He liked that.

Her hips were round and full.

He liked that even more.

"Tell me if you don't like what I'm doing," he whispered. He was desperate to please her. Suddenly, he felt inadequate. It was almost as if his life experiences hadn't prepared him for this moment.

"So far, so good." She rolled her hips, encouraging him to continue.

His sex life with Serena hadn't been good in the last five years. As a matter of fact, it had been two years since they'd even had sex. Well, she'd been getting it somewhere else, while he chose to be faithful. Even when he'd found out, he didn't want his son to see him as a cheater.

With Zinny in his arms, he'd come alive for the first time in years. His pulse raced with enthusiasm.

But his mind reminded him of all his shortcomings.

She threaded her fingers through his hair as he glanced up, catching her gaze. She smiled.

Jesus. She'd sucker punched his heart. He swallowed his breath, watching her expression as he eased his fingers inside, her body ripe and ready.

"Yes," she said with a throaty whisper.

He ducked his head between her legs, letting himself have a quick taste.

"Oh, God." She jerked her hips.

It would take all his resolve to take his time and bask in the pure delight of Zinny.

She grabbed a chunk of his hair and dug her heels into his back. Her soft moans filled the room. Her body moved against his mouth, showing him the way to give her the most pleasure.

And it didn't take long for her orgasm to wet his tongue. She tasted like a strawberry smoothie with whipped cream on top.

He couldn't get enough and he didn't want to stop, but she yanked his hair.

Hard.

"Hey." He blinked, staring at her as he licked his lips.

"Kiss me," she demanded, grabbing his face and bringing his mouth to hers. It was so erotic he thought he might pass out from being so dizzy.

The need to be inside her was too great. He positioned himself between her legs.

"Wait." She gripped his shoulders. "You need to wear a condom."

"Oh. I didn't think about that. It's been a long time since I've had to."

"Yeah. Well. I'm not on any birth control right now. But I can go see the doctor and get some since this should become a regular thing." She reached over to the nightstand and grabbed a condom, handing it to him.

"I'm honestly thrilled you have one, but I'm very jealous of whoever you bought these for."

"Actually, I just picked up that box this week in hopes this might happen."

He stared at her for moment, his jaw dangling open as he contemplated that thought. "You weren't the only one thinking about—imagining what this might be like." He tore the wrapper open with his teeth and quickly covered himself. He thrust deep inside, holding himself steady for a long moment. His lungs burned with rapture. He fanned her cheeks with his thumbs, staring deep into her warm green eyes.

He kissed her mouth. Slowly at first. Tenderly. With as much control as he could muster. He rocked against her body, his restraint diminishing with every stroke.

Everything he thought he understood about women —about relationships—he'd realized in this moment were simply stepping-stones.

"Toby. Yes." She kissed him. Hard. Their tongues twisted and turned in a fever, matching their writhing bodies.

Her climax coaxed his to detonate.

It was as if the room lit up like the Fourth of July.

Her legs wrapped around his waist, squeezing tight.

He buried his face in her neck, gasping for air. He'd heard the men describe mind-blowing sex before and he chalked it up to assholes bragging.

And he still figured that was the case because he'd never in a million years reduce a woman as special as Zinfandel River to a bedroom experience. At least not with anyone else. She wasn't a notch on his belt.

If he never had the experience again, he'd cherish this in his heart forever.

She had a way of restoring his faith in all things good.

He sighed, shifting his weight to the side and pulling the covers over their bodies. He wrapped his arms around her and kissed her forehead.

She snuggled in close, with her knee between his legs and her head on his chest.

It felt like the most natural thing in the world to be with Zinny. It wasn't strange. There was no regret. No afterthought.

Except one.

And he would have to deal with it.

He took in a deep cleansing breath. He didn't want this to end. But he didn't want it under a microscope. He didn't want people judging. Not during a divorce. And not while Serena was going through a trial.

That was the last thing TJ needed.

Zinny lifted her head and rested it on her hands. She smiled.

"You're amazing."

"Thank you," she said. "You're not so bad yourself."

"You might think different after this."

"You don't want anyone to know," she said as if she could read his thoughts.

"It's not because I'd be ashamed of us or anything because—"

She pressed her finger to his lips. "You're going

through a divorce. And Serena is in jail. You're worried about TJ. I get it. I'm also a little worried how my parents and family will react, so I'm happy to keep this between us and not because I want to hide, but because I want to know exactly what it is before we share it with others. Besides, we do have TJ to consider. I shouldn't assume anything, but I'm guessing you don't want to just introduce a woman in his life."

He laughed. "You're kind of already in his life, but no. Not romantically and not this quick. You're right about that." He pushed out a puff of air. "My life is complicated right now."

"I don't want to make it worse."

"I know." He ran his thumb over her lower lip. "For now, whatever this is, we keep it between us."

"Believe it or not, I can be discreet." She laughed. "Have you ever known any of my boyfriends?"

"As a matter of fact, other than that idiot you dated in high school who I caught you necking with on my sofa when you were babysitting, no."

"He was an idiot." She rolled her eyes. "But my relationships are my business and until whoever I'm dating and I are ready to make it anyone else's busi- ness, I don't feel the need to flaunt it."

"Zinfandel River, you are unique."

"So I've been told." She adjusted the covers. "But if we really want to make sure we keep this secret, you shouldn't stay the night. My parents will be up at the crack of dawn, and they will see your car is still in their driveway."

"I should probably go now as they could still be awake." He swung his legs to the side of the bed. His skin chilled from the air-conditioning smacking it. He didn't want to leave her, but he needed to. He found his underwear and pants and hiked them up to his hips. He turned and stared at her as she sat cross-legged on her bed, the sheets barely covering her body, her fiery-red hair flowing over her shoulders.

Her green eyes dancing with delight.

He planted his hands on his hips. "You don't make walking out of this room easy."

"That's the point." She lowered the sheet.

He groaned. "Please don't do that again. I don't want to be chased out of this vineyard by one or both of your parents with a loaded shotgun."

"Yeah. That would suck for you."

"Not helping." He found his shirt and pulled it over his head. He leaned in and kissed her plump, sweet lips. "I'm going to be at the office all day, but do you want to come over and have dinner with me and TJ?" It wasn't like she hadn't been over before. And TJ always enjoyed her company.

"Did you still want me to drive him back and forth to school?"

"I can take him, but if you don't mind picking him up and taking him to the rink for practice, that would be great."

"I don't mind at all."

"Perfect." He took her mouth one more time, letting this one linger longer than he should. It took every ounce of energy he had to pull away. But he had to. He had a long road ahead of him and whatever this was, he had time to figure it out. "I'll pick up steaks on my way home."

"I'll bring a bottle of red."

"I'd rather have a bottle of you."

"Oh, that's so corny." She laughed.

"Yeah. Not one of my better lines." He found his shoes and slipped his feet into them as he padded to the door. He turned and soaked in one last look. "Good night, Zinny."

"Good night, Toby."

He slipped out into the night, wondering how he'd gotten so lucky when he'd thought his world had turned upside down.

2

———

ZINNY

Zinny finished clearing the dinner dishes and brought them into the kitchen. She stood in front of the sink and started rinsing before loading the dishwasher.

"What are you doing?" Toby asked as he came up behind her, wrapping his arms around her and kissing her neck.

She closed her eyes and leaned back, taking in a deep breath, enjoying the stolen moment. "Where's TJ?"

"Taking the trash and recycle to the street."

She turned, snuggling in, stealing a brief passionate kiss, keeping her ears open for the back door.

About fifteen seconds later, it opened.

Toby took a step back, wiping his mouth. He winked.

It had been a week since they slept together, and she wondered if it was going to happen again. His days were filled with work, and it was impossible for him to take time off right now. She tried to entice him with sexy texts in the morning to see if he could meet her for lunch, but he couldn't even do that most days. And other than a kiss here and there, and two dinners, she expected things wouldn't heat up for a while again.

"Hey, Dad," TJ called. "I need the new iTunes password. For some reason it's not saved on the downstairs computer."

"I don't usually give him any of the passwords." Toby sighed. "I bought new phones for us back when Serena moved out. All new accounts. I needed to separate everything. I've changed the password twice. I'm being paranoid."

"No. You're being smart," Zinny said.

"Dad?" TJ stepped into the kitchen. "Can you either give it to me or come into the den and enter it?"

"You can't give this out—"

"I'm not going to," TJ interrupted his father. He rolled his eyes.

Zinny wanted to laugh, but instead, she managed to keep a straight face, something her father had never been too good at when it came to her childhood. Her dad told her he'd been able to do it with her older siblings, but never her and it drove her mom crazy.

"Okay. It's BOSTON39!RiverSt," Toby said.

TJ narrowed his stare. "I get Boston. That's where you went to college and 39 was your hockey number, but what's River St stand for?"

"My senior year I lived off campus and that was the name of the street." Toby ducked his head in the fridge and snagged a beer, offering one to Zinny.

She thought about it for about a half a second, then nodded.

"Really? I thought maybe it was for Zinny. It is her last name." TJ smiled like he knew something everyone else in the room didn't.

That's what Zinny was afraid of. She took a chug of her beer.

"Nope." Toby laughed. "I have a box full of stuff in the attic, and I believe I still have the street sign I stole."

"Real mature, Dad." TJ turned and strolled toward the den, laughing.

"River street? Seriously? Or can I let that one go to my head?"

Toby lifted his beverage. His lips curled over the longneck, and he sipped. His Adam's apple bobbed up and down as he swallowed.

Zinny had it bad.

"I feel a little bad bursting your bubble, but I lived on River Street with three other hockey players. It was a hellhole. Probably the most disgusting place I've ever lived, so, really, you don't want to associate it with your beautiful name." He lowered his gaze slowly, as if he were undressing her. "Or the rest of you."

"You're making me all tingly."

He chuckled. "I think I might have to take you up on lunch tomorrow, but that feels so cheap."

"Are you kidding me? It's sexy. Hot."

"In some ways, it is. But there's a part of me that feels like if we have to sneak around, then we shouldn't be doing it."

"You sound like my mother," Zinny said with an arched brow. "She used to give me that lecture all the time and I'd toss back at her how she'd done that her entire life."

"You're not helping the cause," he said.

"Why do you have to overanalyze everything? Why can't we just enjoy this?" She set the dish towel on the counter, took her beer, and dragged him to the back patio where they wouldn't have to worry about TJ overhearing the conversation.

The warm New Jersey air coated her skin. June could be a crapshoot when it came to weather.

She adjusted her chair while Toby lit the fire pit. The moon and the stars filled the dark sky. Leaning back, she stretched out her legs and soaked up the ambiance. Toby lived on the outskirts of town in one of the nicer neighborhoods. His house used to be overstated, but Serena took all the pretentiousness with her when she moved out.

Toby tapped her shoulder as he sat back. "I don't

want this to be about a quickie in the back seat, hoping someone doesn't catch us like we're doing something wrong, and that's how it feels when you start talking. I'm a little old-fashioned and I don't want to treat you like you're a piece of meat."

"You're not and trust me, I'll either walk out that door or tell you if you are." She glanced over his shoulder and took his hand. "You've been nothing but kind and sweet and insanely respectful of me."

"There's more to it than that." Toby tugged his hand away and shifted his chair so he faced her. "I have TJ to consider. Growing up, my role models for relationships sucked. My parents only showed me what a bad one looked like and I mimicked that something good."

"It's not like my parents have a traditional marriage. Hell, they aren't even married. They had three kids after they got divorced. There isn't anything normal about that." Zinny understood where Toby was coming from. She really did. But he couldn't change the past. He couldn't fix his parents' broken relationship.

Nor could he change what happened between him and Serena. All he could do was be a better man moving forward.

"I get that, but they are kind and decent people who worked together. My parents couldn't do that, and Serena and I screwed up royally. I don't want to do that anymore."

She wanted to reach out and hold him, but she

knew this wasn't the time or place. They needed to be completely alone and that wasn't going to happen until TJ spent the night with his grandma. That usually happened once a week. TJ was a good boy to humor his grandma that way. And he seemed to still enjoy it.

Toby's mom had gone from an angry, bitter old woman to a kinder, gentler version of that. She was still bitter. But her frustration over her life had dissipated.

"You're not. You're an excellent father."

"Sometimes I don't think so."

"Well, you are," Zinny said. "And what you're going through is temporary."

"Now you sound like your father."

Zinny smiled. "I've got the best of both my parents." She leaned forward, pushing her breasts together.

Toby groaned. "You're the devil thought."

She laughed. "So, lunch tomorrow?"

"Oh yeah. It's a date."

Toby

Toby sat at the outside table of the Green Bean Coffee House, sipping his black coffee, nibbling on his blueberry muffin, waiting for Carter River. His cell buzzed.

Zinny: *So you don't forget about me. Kisses.*

Toby blushed. He clutched his cell to his chest and glanced around. Thank God, Carter was nowhere in sight.

Toby's pulse pounded in his ears. Never in his life had anyone sent him sexy pictures before.

Quickly, he stole another glance.

Holy shit.

Zinny wasn't your average sexy woman.

Striking.

Stunning.

Alluring.

Bewitching.

And a million other descriptors.

But what got him all hot and bothered wasn't her good looks. That got his attention. But what held it was her personality. Some people found her brash. Harsh.

He found her honest. Real.

He sighed. He needed to delete the picture. He couldn't afford for anyone to find it on his phone. Not just for his sake. Or his son's.

But for Zinny.

That wouldn't be fair to her.

Toby: *That got my morning off to an interesting start… right before I have to meet with your dad. Hope you have a good day. See you at the rink after work. Thanks for picking up TJ.*

He quickly deleted the picture and none too soon as Carter strolled through the crowd, carrying his own coffee and egg sandwich.

Toby's cheeks had to be five shades of red.

"Good morning, Toby."

"Sir," Toby said. "How are you?"

"I'm well, and you?" Carter took a seat and opened his breakfast sandwich, taking a large bite.

The small talk was torture, but what else was Toby going to do. "I'm honestly kind of worried about everything."

"Well, don't be." Carter took a long sip of his coffee. "She's not contesting the divorce or anything there. You get to keep the house and she's not arguing with division of the rest of the assets."

"That's what concerns me. She's not an agreeable kind of woman."

Carter nodded. "I'm sure she's using that as a ploy or some kind of leverage to get something else she wants."

"Like custody," Toby said.

"We can't do anything about that until after the trial and you can't fill your mind with all the possible bad outcomes." Carter lowered his chin. "Don't get mad at my daughter, because I had to practically browbeat it out of her, but she said that's about all you think about."

Toby needed to have a conversation with Zinny about discussing anything with her dad, but then again, perhaps it wasn't a big deal. Maybe he was reading into something that wasn't there. The entire town knew Zinny was helping him out. He needed a nanny, not a full-time one, but one who could drive.

She'd been a babysitter before college, and sometimes after.

It made sense.

To him.

Hopefully, it did to the rest of the world.

"My son is everything to me. I can't lose him, and with Serena not taking the plea, it means she could be found not guilty."

"That doesn't mean you won't be granted full custody. We have a litany of things Serena has done throughout your marriage that proves her parenting skills are questionable."

"And she has a list on me," Toby said. "Let's be honest. I've been an asshole in the past."

Carter wiped his fingers on his napkin and leaned back. "I spent this last week chatting with people in town, and everyone I spoke to all agreed that when it comes to hockey, you could be intense and hard on TJ. Maybe too hard. However, everyone switched right over to Serena and how much worse she was and how she would belittle TJ and you even occasionally had to remove her from the stands."

"That doesn't negate what I did." Toby wouldn't deny that he believed one hundred percent that he was the better parent.

"Toby. I wish I had videotape of you. The worst thing you ever did to TJ as a hockey dad was expect him to be better than he is or maybe you lived a little through him." Carter leaned forward, palming his paper coffee mug. "Weezer and I are guilty of the same thing. We ran our four older children right out of our business and out of town. We're lucky we didn't run them right out of our lives. Riesling didn't even want to bring her daughter around us because of the way Weezer behaved. When Dax came back into town, it stirred up your inadequacies as a hockey player and you projected that onto your son. But Dax, Chablis, and Zinny were all there during the showcase and you didn't behave as badly toward your kid as you think you did. Your behavior was directed at Dax, but it came out sideways because of what you and Serena were going through at the time. Toss in Brooks, and you were a hot mess."

"You're making excuses for me."

"No. I'm not." Carter shook his head. "I'm giving you the chance to be human and I want you to spend more time reminding yourself what a selfless father you are instead of holding on to your mistakes. If I did that, I might as well bury myself in the vineyard and call it a day."

Toby chuckled. "I see your point."

"Good." Carter nodded. "So, I really want you at Serena's hearing for the trial date. Can you be there?"

"I've taken the day off work and Zinny said she can take care of TJ that day. I know he's fourteen and can be alone, but on a day like that, I don't want him to be."

"I was going to suggest that he come to our house,

but having Zinny works since she's a familiar face." Carter's gaze dropped to his disposable cup. He lifted it and swirled the liquid. "You rely heavily on my daughter."

"I don't know what TJ and I would do without her." Toby's breath stuck in his chest. It felt like an elephant had climbed on his body and wouldn't get off. "If it's too much because of her new position at the vineyard, I can look for other help. It's just that my mom can't drive anymore and—"

Carter held up his hand. "No. Zinny's perfectly capable of juggling. She's like her mother that way. I have no idea how either one does it and I get dizzy watching them, but Zinny thrives on being busy. Besides, if she was idle, she'd be finding projects for me to do around the house and vineyard and right before harvest, I'm just not in the mood."

"She dropped TJ off last night and told me I needed to paint the living room. She thought it looked foggy."

Carter burst out laughing. "If she said that, today she'll show up with paint cans for you."

"Well, she can bring them all she wants. I'm not painting the living room."

"Oh. You don't know her that well then because she'll roll up her sleeves and demand you do it with her. And she won't take no for an answer," Carter said. "It doesn't matter that it's not her house and not her business." Carter stood. "She's made you and TJ her business and she's going to stick it out because she cares. My wife says if she wants to help me with something it's because she cares." Carter glanced at his watch. "I've got to get going. I'll talk to you later."

Toby blew out a puff of air.

He knew Zinny cared. A lot. He cared about her too.

He just didn't like the fact that people—specifically her father—were noticing.

3

ZINNY

Zinny blinked open her eyes and inhaled sharply. The fresh scent of Toby filled her lungs.

But that couldn't be. He was supposed to—shit.

They'd fallen asleep. "Toby." She pressed her hand on his chest and gave him a gentle wiggle.

"Huh?" He wrapped his arm around her shoulder and pulled her closer. "Is it morning—oh crap." He pushed to a sitting position and wiped his eyes.

In the few weeks they'd been dating, she'd never had the privilege of waking up to him and he was damn cute when he was all flustered.

"What time is it?" he asked.

"Well, it's still darkish outside."

"It's the ish part that concerns me." He reached across her and snagged his phone. "It's almost five. Your parents will be awake soon. I can't afford to have them see me driving away. Last week when I had breakfast with your dad, he made all sorts of comments about what caring meant."

"My dad was just being his usual self," she said. "But my family isn't the enemy. We don't have to—"

"Until this trial and my divorce is settled, this is the way it has to be." He cupped the back of her neck and gave her a big kiss.

One with intent.

One that reminded her that even though this was still new, he wasn't using her. She believed that ninety-five percent of the time. It wasn't so much that he was ridiculously adamant about secrecy that bothered her, but how he worried about the little things.

Like their age.

Or what people were going to think about that one thing and how it looked on the outside. It shouldn't matter and that's what bothered her because it felt more like his concern came from Serena's influence than who Toby was as his own man.

"When that is over, and TJ has had some time to adjust to all of this, I'll face the firing squad."

"My family isn't that bad."

"Your mother is going to hang me if your father doesn't shoot me first." He pressed his finger against her lips. "I need to go clean up before I race home, change, and then pick up TJ at my mom's."

"Do you think TJ would notice you're wearing the same thing from yesterday?"

"Probably not, but my mom would, and she would say something. I don't need TJ commenting. He's noticing things just like your dad is." He yanked the covers back and strode toward the bathroom.

"I'll put on a pot of coffee."

"I'd much appreciate that." He waved his hand over his head before shutting the door.

She found the T-shirt she'd stolen of his and a pair of boxers he'd left behind that she'd never returned after cleaning them. It had been an immature move, but she didn't care. Part of her wondered how long this affair would last. It wasn't the age difference that concerned her.

Or her parents.

Toby made a big deal about that, but they could be the exact same age and he'd still be frightened of her mother. And her dad.

Especially her father.

Of all the River kids, she was daddy's little girl.

The baby of the family. And while she didn't think any of her siblings were planned, she was a big shock to her parents. But as her father always told her, Zinny was one of the most exciting things that had ever happened.

He said something special about all his kids. So did her mom; however, Zinny was the last one and she'd been a little spoiled.

She knew it, her siblings knew it, and she wasn't

about to apologize for it. Unfortunately, it's why she always kept her love life to herself.

Reaching to the right of the stove, she found one of those pod things. She'd never been a big regular coffee drinker, but she made sure she kept a small stash for when her siblings showed up.

She placed it in the machine and hit the button.

Staring at it, she tapped her foot, watching it fill and inhaling sharply. She liked the smell, but preferred a sweet drink from the Green Bean filled with sugar and caffeine. One thing she didn't like about living back at the winery was that on the days she spent working from home, driving into town for her morning beverage meant judgment from her mother for taking the time when she could be spending those minutes crunching numbers or learning more about the business.

Then came the lectures on why Zinny should just quit her other job.

Well, she wasn't ready to make that full commitment yet. It would be a pay cut for one. It didn't matter that she was living rent free. She liked making her own money and she liked putting it in the bank.

Toby appeared wearing his clothes and a weak smile. "I hate this as much as you do."

She leaned against the counter and handed him his fresh mug.

"But even if I wasn't going through all this with Serena, I have TJ to consider."

"Toby, you don't have to explain. I get it." And she

did. Not to mention everyone would judge their age difference. There would be gossip. She would walk into the beauty parlor and everyone would stare at her and then turn their heads and whisper behind her back.

Of course, she was used to that.

She was the Weezer's daughter after all.

People chatted about that all the time.

All the secrets that kept getting dug up about her family. Or the unconventional way her parents had raised their children. Small towns were full of small minds who loved to gossip.

"I think we need to talk about this." Toby lifted the cup to his lips. He blew for a long moment before taking a slow sip.

This was it.

He'd had some time to think and he was going to end it and she couldn't argue. Not if he brought TJ into the conversation. TJ was just a kid who was going through a lot of changes. Her teenage years were nothing compared to what that kid had to deal with. But he also needed people in his life who could lift him up. Support him. Love him.

She fit that bill.

"I'm listening."

"I'm not used to you being this quiet." Toby set the mug on the island. He locked gazes with Zinny. "When I walked out of here the first night, I was so torn. I couldn't believe I had let anything happen between us. I didn't understand where it was coming from and I swore to myself when I saw you the next day, we'd end it. But I couldn't."

She braced herself both physically and emotionally for his next words. She didn't think this would hurt this much, but her heart had already begun to crack.

"This thing with us has been so easy, but it's happening so fast my head is spinning and the worst part is all we ever do is hide out here or at my place whenever TJ spends the night at my parents' or at a friend's, which has only happened three times."

"You're not used to me keeping my mouth shut. Well, you're rambling and I have no idea what the point is and you're making me nervous." She went right for the fridge, ducked her head inside, and snagged a diet soda.

Loaded.

She cracked it open, found a straw, and started sucking.

Toby laughed. "That's not a strawberry frappe-something or other."

"Just keep talking, pal."

"All right," he said. "My point is that TJ will be moving into the dorms for hockey camp in two weeks."

"The other day you were on the fence about letting him move in for the summer. You said not all the team members were doing it."

"I was mistaken," Toby said. "Dax informed me that the entire team committed to the camp and I don't want TJ ostracized any more than he already feels because of what is going on with his mom. My only concern is her showing up before this damn trial is over."

The trial hadn't even been scheduled yet. That would happen next week since Serena had turned down the plea bargain offer. Zinny's father hadn't loved the plea agreement since there would be no jail time served, but it would be an admission of guilt and it would help Toby with his case for physical custody.

Going to trial was always a risk, but the case was strong and she would likely be convicted. The only question then became what the sentence would be. That all came down to the judge.

"So, what are you getting at?" Zinny asked. Her mind went from being dumped to a romantic getaway to a summer of sex to right back to being dumped because it was just sex.

"Between now and the hearing, I need your help with TJ."

"I told you that I can pick him up from school and bring him back to your office or the winery or wherever. It's no big deal."

"I appreciate that. My mom—"

"Toby. I'm here for you and TJ. Even if we're not doing this, I'm not going to bail on him."

Toby curled his fingers around her biceps and squeezed. "I want to spend as much time as possible with him before I move him into the dorms. I know he's only going to be living a few miles away and Dax was kind enough to give me the manager job for the team, so I'll have a real active role and will see him all the time. But it's different."

"Are you asking me to take a step back?"

He palmed her cheek. "Not so much that as I'm not going to be letting him have sleepovers anymore. I'm going to take him camping next weekend. And movies every night. He's my only child and I feel like my heart is being ripped from my chest."

She inched closer and wrapped her arms around Toby's waist, resting her head on his chest. "You're going to bawl like a baby when that kid goes to college."

"Oh yeah, I am."

"You're a good father."

He pressed his lips against the top of her head. "Thanks for understanding. Maybe when he's all settled in his room, you and I can go away where no one knows who we are and we can be a normal couple."

A couple.

Butterflies filled her stomach.

"I'd like that." She lifted her gaze. "Can we go to Lake George? Or maybe Saratoga Springs?"

"Sure. I'll set something up."

She melted into his goodbye kiss that lingered for a couple of minutes too long. "You better go."

"I'll text you later." He lifted his finger. "Do not

send me dirty texts at work. You're killing me with those."

"What, you don't like my breasts?" She lifted her shirt, giving him a little peek.

He groaned. "Those are really nice, but such a distraction when I'm on a conference call."

"Let me know your schedule and I'll send something between—"

He hushed her by pressing his hand over her mouth. "I have their image ingrained permanently in my brain. It's not necessary."

She laughed. "But it's so much fun."

"I have to ask. Have you sent boob pictures to other boyfriends?"

"Are you my boyfriend? Is that what we're calling this?"

He sighed. "Sometimes you're exhausting. Answer my question."

"No. You're the first."

"And I hope to be the last and only." He kissed her nose. "I better get out of here before it gets too late." He turned on his heel and sauntered toward the door. He glanced over his shoulder. "You're something else, Zinny."

"Have a good day." She wiggled her fingers and smiled.

He disappeared out the door.

She slid down and sat on the cold, hard floor, covering her face. The relationships she'd had in the past were good. She enjoyed them. And she cared for the men she'd dated.

But they weren't Toby.

She could admit, if only to herself, that she'd had a crush on him for years. But in the last year that crush changed to real, bona fide feelings. Having acted on them, they'd grown into something she'd never experienced before. It wasn't infatuation, but she didn't dare call it anything other than the most real and grown-up affair she'd ever been in. It had potential to be the real thing.

The one.

She'd have to go find all the bullets to her mother's shotgun and hide them.

Carter

Carter stood in front of the master bedroom picture window and sipped his coffee while he stared out over the vineyards. They were still two months away from harvest, but this was a crucial time. However, Eliza Jane was due to give birth in the next four weeks and Malbec had mentioned she was miserable. Her false labor pains were getting worse, so Merlot and Chablis were picking up the slack by doing the early morning walks.

And Carter and Weezer were doing some too.

Just like they used to do when they'd first gotten married.

"That window looks good on you," Weezer said as she stepped from the bathroom. The smell of her lilac soap followed her along with the warmth of her shower.

"It does feel good to be living here full-time." He wasn't sure about it at first. The last thirty years of their marriage—well, divorce—had been under separate roofs and they'd done just fine. Better than fine. They thrived. They were closer than ever and he didn't want to screw that up.

Weezer was the only person he ever wanted to grow old with and he didn't care if he had to do it by packing an overnight bag occasionally. Besides, they were both the kind of people who needed their space. He would need to be respectful and mindful of whenever Weezer needed a moment.

Or when he had to take one.

She came up behind him and wrapped her arms around his waist. She kissed his shoulder. "Whose car is that driving away from the cottage?"

"It's Toby's." Carter sighed. He'd been worried about what had been brewing between Toby and his youngest child. He'd kept his mouth closed for the most part, with the exception of a few dropped hints that no one commented on. Of all his children, Zinny was the most like his wife. If he confronted Zinny about what was going on, she'd do one of two things.

Tell him exactly what he didn't want to hear and then to mind his own fucking business.

Or she'd dig her heels in and shut him out.

Neither option was acceptable. Especially when he was Toby's lawyer and his baby girl obviously cared for the man.

Man.

Jesus. He was the same age as Malbec, Carter's oldest child who had turned seventeen when Zinny had been born. Carter could try to justify in his mind that Toby was six months younger, but that didn't really help.

Sixteen years was a big age difference.

And there was a fourteen-year-old child involved.

Most people looked at Zinny and saw this wildly energetic young lady who had barely lived. But if that's all they saw, then they didn't see the real woman. She might come across as inexperienced, but she had an old soul and she was wise beyond her years.

She was simply a product of her generation.

And of him and Weezer.

The latter made him smile.

He was proud of his family and who they had all become. Each one of his children—in spite of how he and Weezer had fucked them up—turned out to be incredible people capable of greatness.

Weezer raised up on tiptoe and peered over his shoulder. "Why is he here at five forty in the morning?"

"You don't want to know, dear." Carter and Weezer had promised each other no more lies. No more secrets. Not between them. The one her father and grandfather made her keep from him regarding how her family stole this winery from Eliza Jane's could have destroyed everything. As much as he didn't think it was a good idea for Weezer to know what he did, it would be worse for him if he kept it from the love of his life.

"Carter River. You better tell me what the hell is going on, or you're going to find yourself sleeping in the guest room."

He wrapped his arm around her shoulders and held her tight to his body. "You have to promise me you're not going to go off half-cocked."

"How about fully loaded."

He chuckled. "Nope. You can't do that either."

"Fuck," she mumbled. "He slept there last night, didn't he," she said with a long breath. She pushed from Carter's embrace and turned. Planting her hands on her hips, she shook her head. "I can't say I didn't know she liked him."

"We both saw how he looked at her during the family dinner a few weeks ago." Carter set his coffee on the dresser and ran a hand over the top of his head.

"I didn't think Toby would pursue her." Weezer turned. "To be honest, I'm not concerned about the age difference. She's a grown woman. Inexperienced about some things in life and she tends to jump into every-thing she does with two feet, but that's part of what makes her so special."

Carter couldn't disagree, though he did struggle with how much older Toby was. That was his baby girl. Nothing could change that.

"But Toby has baggage, and I'm not talking about his son," Weezer said. "I love that kid. He's funny and I would hate it if he didn't come around here anymore. He's quite inquisitive and he's not afraid of me."

"That's the first time anyone under the age of eighteen wasn't terrified of you," he said with a chuckle. "But this whole thing with Serena is terrible, and Toby is forever tied to her because of TJ. The truly sad part is Toby will always end up giving her the benefit of the doubt because she's his mother."

Carter couldn't say too much about what he knew regarding the divorce and what Toby desired in custody and visitation. Toby didn't want to take TJ from his mother, but he did want incredibly strict boundaries.

The biggest one being that Serena didn't get to make decisions regarding anything major in TJ's life.

The next one being that Brooks was not to be involved or around TJ.

And finally, her visits were restricted to no overnights.

Carter didn't think the latter would be granted. But it was possible considering some of Serena's question-able choices.

"It's going to be impossible now for me to keep my mouth closed," Weezer said. "I'm sure you want to say something to Zinny about this."

"Of course I do. But we can't. Not right now anyway." Carter closed the gap and took Weezer by the forearms. "Zinny and Toby are keeping this private."

"He just drove off our property. That's not being discreet."

"Sure, it is," he said. "No one is here but us this early and we're not going to say anything. Besides, there's nothing wrong with what they are doing." He closed his eyes for a moment and let that thought sink in. "I just worry about when it does come out—because it will—what it will look like for Toby and how it will make our daughter look."

"Do you think they should get ahead of it? Because I'll march down to the carriage house and—"

He pressed his finger on Weezer's lips. "No. Not until after the trial. Maybe after that is over and then final custody is settled, then they can go out on a date in public. But until then, I'll drop a gentle reminder to Zinny about how important it is to keep her personal life out of the headlines."

"You might as well tell her that you know, which means, we can have the conversation."

"Weezer. Stop." He arched a brow. "Trust me on this. If we go telling Zinny what to do and how to do it, she's going to do exactly what you would do, and do you want that?"

She pursed her lips as if she just ate a sour lemon. "Fine. You make a valid point."

"Good. Now let's go for a stroll through the vineyards and then grab some breakfast." During his walk around the property, he'd come up with some great one-liners or cute stories that would get his point across to Zinny without letting her know they saw Toby basically do the walk of shame.

4

———

TOBY

Toby sat in the stands with a thick binder and a cup of coffee. He glanced down at the ice. TJ hadn't been having the best practice, but Dax had been going on easy on him, without playing favorites. Toby was truly impressed with Dax's coaching skills.

And his compassion.

Of course, TJ was just a kid. He didn't deserve to have the world treat him poorly because his parents were assholes.

Toby called himself that because of the way he'd acted over the years, especially when it came to hockey. He realized that his marital problems had influenced how he treated people.

Something he needed to change.

He'd been so angry for so long.

His cell vibrated. He pulled it out of his pocket and smiled.

Zinny: *Just an FYI. I'll be at the rink at 5. TJ left his back-pack in my car. He has his final exams next week and I think it's safe to assume he needs to study.*

Toby: *Thank you. He sure does.*

He let his fingers hover over the keyboard before he hit send while he contemplated his thoughts. He shouldn't do it. But what harm could it do? It wasn't like the entire town didn't know that Zinfandel River was working three jobs.

The family winery.

Selling wine.

And his part-time nanny when he couldn't leave work.

They didn't hide that. It was their affection for one another that he needed to keep a secret.

Even from his son.

But that didn't mean he couldn't invite her to pizza night.

Toby: *We're going to grab some pizza for dinner in town. Want to join us?*

Zinny: *You know I do. But only if you don't think it will get people talking.*

He chuckled. So far, he hadn't heard a word. And he'd been spending a fair amount of time with her. That had to be a good sign. Someone would have said something if people were whispering behind his back.

Toby: *I think it's fine.*

Zinny: *Perfect. Pizza it is.*

He put his cell in his back pocket and went back to

this insane binder that Dax had put together. Talk about details. Holy shit. For the upperclassmen and those who had been on the team before, there were stats from every game they had ever played for Candlewood Falls Prep. It also had notes from their previous coach about strengths and weaknesses.

Of course, Dax had put in the margins whether or not he agreed with those assessments.

For the new players, which there were three including TJ, Dax had compiled a history taken from their last two seasons, and it was specific. Toby was impressed with the thought that had gone into it.

And the accuracy.

But he sure as hell didn't like to see in black-and-white what he'd turned his son into. It was going to take some seriously good coaching to turn that ship around. TJ had been trained to be a selfish player. A one-man show in part because he was one of the better kids on the ice and that was apparent.

But that didn't win games.

That only got you ostracized by both players and coaches.

A lesson that Toby had forgotten.

Of course, his problem had been being in Dax's shadow. Only, Toby had been the one to put himself there. No one else did that. Well, his father had helped.

He needed to stop focusing on that. Things were changing. He'd given up a lot of control and if he proved he could play nice, Dax would let him on the bench since he needed another registered coach, but he wasn't willing to name Toby just yet.

At least Dax was honest in how he felt and that he didn't trust Toby.

That was understandable. It had only been six weeks since Serena had been arrested and Toby turned over his new leaf.

He shifted his gaze to the ice. Dax had the boys doing a scrimmage and he had TJ on defense.

Toby bit his tongue. TJ wasn't a defenseman. But he could play point. Dax had warned Toby that he would do things that Toby didn't like.

This was one of them.

But Toby did trust Dax and learning what the defense needed to do could only help TJ be a better hockey player. This wasn't a game and even it was, TJ was the new kid on the block and he wasn't going to be a starter. Toby had to accept that.

This new and improved man took work.

Out of the corner of his eye he saw Serena strolling through the arena toward the corner of the rink.

Fuck.

He should have known she wouldn't respect his wishes long. Hopping to his feet, he took the bleachers two at a time while telling himself he wasn't going to cause a scene. And if she did, he'd be the bigger person and remain calm.

Did he even know how to do that when it came to Serena?

His skin prickled with heat.

It was hard to believe that at one time he loved her. Or maybe he loved the idea of her because she'd come back into his life right after his father had died. He'd hoped that maybe he and his dad could have a moment before his dad left this earth. Something that would give Toby an inclination that he wasn't a total disappointment to his father.

But hours before his dad died, he told Toby once again that Toby had never quite lived up to what a son should be and that Charlie was going to go to his grave with a broken heart because his son was a shit.

Today, Toby knew his father projected his own failures onto him and that he wasn't a failure. But when presented with the opportunity to raise a child and do right by them, he took it.

Serena, at first, was so sweet and kind. Not the same crazy teenaged girl who used to do horrible things to Dax because Toby father's paid her to do it.

Like the time she messed with Dax's skate blades.

No. Serena becoming a mom had changed her. For ten years they were happy. Or so Toby thought.

"Serena. What are you doing here?" he asked with a hushed tone, trying to mask his anger.

"I want to see my son." She pushed her dark hair over her shoulders with a calculated flip.

"You can't, so please leave before he sees you."

She folded her arms and started tapping her high-heeled closed-toe shoe. "Seeing him once a week with a therapist around isn't enough. It's cruel and not fair to me. Or to TJ." She tapped the center of her chest. "I'm his mother."

"You should have thought about that before you had an affair and committed a federal crime." He should have kept his mouth shut. This was not the time or place to push her buttons. He cleared his throat. "If you want to set up two visits next week, I'd be open to that as long as it doesn't interfere with his studies. He's got exams—"

"I know what he has." She cocked her head. "And I want to take him to dinner tonight. He needs to know that my mom—his grandma—took a plea bargain. She's going to jail."

"Well, you're not going to see him, and he already knows about his grandma. You and I have gone to court, and this is the visitation for now. I'm going to enforce it."

"What are you going to do? Call the cops on me?"

"Don't force my hand, Serena."

"Do you really want TJ to hate you? Because that's what is going to happen if you do that and he sees them confronting me. He wants to see me and spend time with me. He's scared and confused."

Toby pinched the bridge of his nose. He didn't need a lecture about the changes in his kid. It broke his heart how different TJ had become in the last month. He'd been withdrawn and a little depressed. Right now, the only thing TJ looked forward to was being on the ice with Dax.

And spending time at the winery with Weezer.

That was a bit weird, but if it made the boy happy, then Toby would keep making sure TJ spent time there. Besides, it meant he got to steal a few kisses from a woman who lips were like an angel.

"You need to think about what breaking our agreement will do to your case because it won't look good for you. We can set up a dinner next week, through the proper channels. This is not the right way." He held up his phone. "Don't make me do this."

Slowly, her determined expression turned into an exasperated sigh. "What are you going to do when Brooks starts coming around and wants to get to know *his* son?"

Every single time they got into it, she had to remind him TJ wasn't his biologically and threaten that Brooks was going to all of a sudden want to get to know the child he never wanted.

Toby had to admit to himself that the words stung.

But deep down he knew Brooks wanted nothing to do with TJ. He'd made that perfectly clear. He'd wanted Dax's job and he'd wanted to continue screwing Serena.

But when she got arrested, he ran for the hills.

Toby didn't think he'd ever see the man again.

"You have one minute to turn around and leave or I dial 9-1-1." He wasn't going to take the bait and get into the Brooks debate. He glanced over his shoulder. From where they stood, TJ wouldn't be able to see them from the bench, and currently, that's where he was, but there would be a shift change soon, and on the ice, things would be different.

"I'm going to get you for this," she said behind a tight jaw. "You wait. You will pay for what you've done to me and my son." She turned on her heel and stomped toward the lobby just as Zinny came bouncing through the doors.

Fuck.

Serena had always tolerated Zinny as a babysitter because she was always available and TJ liked her when he'd been a toddler. Outside of that, there was no love lost between the two women.

And this would be the first time they'd run into each other since Serena's arrest.

He couldn't imagine Serena would have anything nice to say.

Serena skidded to a stop.

He hightailed it in their direction. Not that Zinny needed his help, but she did have a tendency to put both feet in her mouth.

"What are you doing here?" Serena looked Zinny up and down. She turned. "She better not be here to pick up TJ. Otherwise, that could be me."

"Relax," Zinny said. "I came with my sister." She lifted her hand with her thumb up as if she were hitching a ride and pointed it over her shoulder.

Chablis stood at the office window talking with the person behind the desk, oblivious to what was happening ten feet away.

Toby let his breath fly out of his mouth. He hadn't been aware he'd been holding it.

"Why?" Serena asked.

"I don't have to explain myself to you." Zinny side-stepped Serena, making eye contact. "Good afternoon, Toby. How are you?"

"I'm okay." He swallowed as she walked right on by.

"If I find out she was here to babysit, you're going to regret lying to me." Serena huffed and made her way out of the arena.

"That was unpleasant," he whispered to no one.

"What was she doing here?" Zinny's voice boomed in his ears.

He jumped. "You scared me." He turned, reached out, and squeezed her forearm. "You're early."

"Only a half hour," Zinny said. "Right after I texted you, Chablis asked what I was doing and if I'd be willing to give her a ride. She and Dax are going to some fancy restaurant." She leaned a little closer. "He's going to propose tonight and she's going to say yes."

"And you know this how?"

Zinny laughed. Her smile was bright and her green eyes sparkled like the sun hitting the Caribbean Sea. "I helped Dax pick out the ring."

"That's sweet, but shouldn't we be whispering?"

"I had strict specifications from Chablis. She's not a flashy girl and Dax tends to go too far."

"So, she knows this is coming?"

"She's already started planning the wedding." Zinny reached behind her head and adjusted her ponytail. "Though it will just be a little backyard ceremony, family only in a couple of weeks."

"And does Dax know this?"

"Yeah. They are so weird. I just hope he doesn't do the rink in the cake proposal thing. I wish he could do something she wouldn't see coming, but since she does know it's happening tonight at dinner, I don't see how."

"I also don't see Dax as Mister Romance." Toby placed his hand on the small of her back and guided her toward the bleachers where he left his manager's book. Thankfully, no parents were allowed at practices.

Except him.

The perk of being a manager and hopefully an assistant coach.

"Chablis says he has his moments, but my sister's idea of the perfect romantic moment is being served a cheeseburger in bed."

"I wouldn't mind that." Toby laughed. "Where's TJ's backpack?"

"I left it in my car and right now, I'm glad I did. I'm also even happier Chablis needed a ride. I'm not sure what I would have said to Serena."

"I was a little worried about that."

Zinny pursed her lips. "I wouldn't do anything on purpose to hurt you or TJ."

"I know that." He reached behind her and ran his hand up and down her back for half a minute before he remembered they were in public. "But you do have a razor-sharp tongue and I've never known you to keep your mouth shut. I remember when you were maybe seventeen and babysitting for us and Serena had disciplined TJ in a way that you disapproved of."

"Oh. I remember that afternoon well. The problem was that she disciplined him for something I know he didn't do."

"She blamed you for covering for him," Toby said. "In private, she even wondered if maybe you did it."

"That doesn't surprise me."

"But what I want to know is, how do you know it was her fault? Because we never did get to the bottom of it and I just let it go. It was a small dent and a few tiny scratches. It buffed out well enough. The only thing was it was a brand-new car that we really couldn't afford."

Zinny dropped her head to her knees. "I can't believe I'm going to tell you this."

"You've kept a secret for the last seven years?" He gave her a little shove with his shoulder.

She groaned. "Believe it or not, I can keep my mouth closed. And yes, because I wasn't sure what it meant and it wasn't my business."

"Okay. Well, I'm all ears."

"Merlot was out with Luke Sheridan. Luke had come back to town for a brief visit. They were at a pub over in Hilliard."

"And Serena was there?"

"She was with her parents and she'd been fighting with her dad about money. Merlot didn't pay too much attention until Serena called her father a few choice names and tossed her purse at him. He ducked and it landed on the car. She then went on a rant about how her husband was going to freak out and how badly you treated her."

"That explains a lot." Toby shook his head. "I had asked her dad to stop giving her money for things. Of course, she continued to spend way more than we could afford. She was spoiled."

"You have told my family that for ten years you were in a happy marriage, but that's not what I saw. I'm sorry, Toby. But she's a bitch."

"She can be," Toby admitted. "And these last few years that's all she's been; however, our marriage wasn't all bad. Especially the first five years or so. But she didn't like the idea that I didn't want to be tied to her father. And she hated it even more that her dad enjoyed the idea that I wanted to support my family on my own. I refused his money left and right and that pissed her off, so when she bought that car, I was pissed, and truthfully, that was really the beginning of our problems."

"Can I ask you a really personal question?"

"This coming from the woman who sent me a half-naked picture this morning." His cheeks flushed. "Of course."

"Why didn't you have more kids?"

"I wanted them and I thought we were trying, but about a year after the car incident, I found out she'd been secretly taking birth control. She told me she'd gone in for testing and that she was fine. I went for testing and I was fine. I wanted to go see a specialist and she decided it wasn't meant to be. By this time, TJ was eight and showing a lot of promise in hockey and I turned all my attention to that. My marriage was falling apart and I didn't seem to care. I turned into a man I didn't even recognize."

"Don't be so hard on yourself." She smiled. "We all make mistakes. Look at my mom. She's made some really big ones in her day and yet she walks through town with her head held high and doesn't give a shit what people think."

"I care what you think."

Zinny had a way of turning his heart to mush.

"Then you're in luck. Because I believe you're a pretty swell guy."

"Swell?" He tossed his head back and laughed. She was a surprise a minute.

"Oh, my God. Dax is going to do it here." Zinny poked his arm. "And he's going to use the team to do it."

Toby rested his elbows on his knees and leaned

forward. His heart raced. He remembered his proposal to Serena.

It had been pathetic. He'd wanted to pull out all the stops, but she kept harping on him about how her stomach was getting bigger and bigger and how everyone was going to know they were getting married because she was pregnant.

If they had done the math more closely, everyone would have also figured out he wasn't the father.

But he didn't care.

She did.

And it ruined his night.

He ended up giving her the ring without even asking and she'd never forgotten that fact.

"I've got to get closer." Zinny jumped to her feet and before Toby could even gather his stuff, she was standing at the corner of the rink with her face pressed against the plexiglass.

Chablis had come onto the bench and she stood next to Dax with her hands clutching her chest while the boys skated to the other side, holding signs.

Dax dropped to one knee and held out a box.

Chablis nodded wildly as Dax put the ring on her finger.

The boys turned and held up their signs, which spelled: SHE SAID YES.

The few people in the rink went wild cheering. The hockey team erupted in hoots and chants before skating off to the bench.

Toby laughed as he approached Zinny. He wrapped his arm around her waist.

She dropped her head to his shoulder and sniffled.

"Are you crying?"

"No." She elbowed him. "There's lots of mildew in here and it's bothering my allergies."

"If you say so." He dropped his hand when he made eye contact with his son. It was getting harder and harder to hide his feelings for Zinny.

But he had to.

And not just because of the trial. There would be another custody hearing after that. He didn't think he could be penalized for dating a younger woman, but he had to make sure.

Only, his lawyer happened to be Zinny's father.

That conversation wasn't going to be easy.

But he had a little time before he needed to have it.

"I'm really happy for them," Toby said.

Zinny glanced up with tears welling in her eyes. He wanted to wipe them away, but he couldn't.

That broke his heart.

"They've waited a long time for this moment. I wouldn't be surprised if they got pregnant right away too." She rubbed her hands together. "One more little one for me to practice on."

All the air in his lungs flew out like a jet leaving the runway and soaring straight up through the clouds.

Zinny wanted children of her own.

Toby had just turned forty. Ten years ago, he

thought he wanted at least two more. But that ship had sailed.

He couldn't give Zinny everything she wanted.

Deserved.

That was a fact he had to face and he needed to do it now. If he didn't, he'd only make it worse of all of them, his son included.

Zinny

"I'm so excited for you." Zinny hugged her sister. "I can't believe he did that and we had no idea."

"I'm blown away. It was so sweet." Chablis wiped the tear that ran down her cheek. "We've talked about getting married and starting a family. It's not like this was a surprise." She wiggled her finger. "But boy, was the delivery a huge shocker. Those teenage boys were so giddy it was hysterical."

"They looked like they had a ton of fun with it," Zinny said.

"I saw you and Toby in the corner after. You looked deep in conversation. What's going on with you two?" Chablis lowered her chin. When she did that, she looked like their mother and it drove Zinny crazy.

"What are you talking about?"

"I know you've been TJ's babysitter since you were

like eleven and you've been very kind to that kid all through this."

"He's an innocent child and he needs grown-ups in his life who he can count on. I'm not going to just suddenly abandon the poor kid. Besides, Toby still has to work for a living. He has bills to pay and I don't mind helping out."

"You're awfully defensive which tells me my instincts are correct. I saw it when they came over for Sunday dinner and I keep seeing it. Something is brewing."

Zinny had been told by everyone in her family that she wore her emotions on her sleeve. It had been confirmed by her friends—and especially her boyfriends—that fact had been true. She couldn't hide how she felt. If someone pissed her off, everyone knew. But the one thing she'd always been able to do was keep her relationships private.

When she'd dated Levi Mep, the assistant district attorney, the one who filed the charges against Serena, no one ever knew. If her father had known, he would have had something to say about that. Levi and her dad, while on friendly terms, had gone head-to-head in court a few times.

But the big thing would have been his age.

He was twelve years older than Zinny and when her dad had seen her sharing a cup of coffee with him at the Green Bean, he'd made a big deal about his age and the fact he had a child from his first wife and how those kinds of relationships could be complicated.

That was kind of funny coming from her dad, though neither him nor her mom ever dated other people when they divorced. Nope. They just kept having more kids while they lived in separate houses. If she allowed herself to think about it too much, she could understand why other people thought it was weird.

To her, it made her parents more endearing.

They loved each other so much they did whatever it took to keep their family intacted, even if it was because of lies and secrets from past generations.

"Nothing is going on," she said.

"Right. And I didn't just get officially engaged." Chablis took her by the hands and dragged her through the lobby and out the door.

The warm summer air drenched Zinny's body.

"Come on. You can tell me. I'm not going to say anything to anyone, although people are noticing."

Zinny didn't want to have this conversation, but she figured she had to now that Chablis had brought up other people, whoever they were. "Who is noticing what, exactly?"

"Mom and Dad for starters. They haven't said much, but you have to be blind not to see the way you and Toby look at each other. Malbec asked me about it the other day and so did Riesling."

Okay. That was just family. As long as it wasn't random people gossiping, she could deal with that.

Sort of.

"You can tell everyone to relax. I'm just helping Toby out through the trial and into the custody hearing after that. TJ doesn't need a babysitter, but he doesn't want the kid to be alone all the time, so I'm the logical choice. He's known me since he was a toddler. He trusts me and Toby still has to work and all that. He needs a little help where his mom can't. I can pick him up from school and—"

"Zinny, do you hear yourself?" Chablis held her by the biceps. "Not only are you talking faster than normal, and for you that means faster than a speeding bullet, but you're explaining something to me, your sister, that I already know, which tells me something is definitely going on."

"No. You're jumping to all the wrong conclusions." Zinny pursed her lips and shook her head. Her heart beat so loud it drowned out all her other thoughts.

"You don't need to hide it from me."

Yes, she did. And not because she wanted to keep it to herself, but because Toby asked her to and she had to respect his wishes. She held her sister's gaze for a long moment. She opened her mouth to say something —anything—but she couldn't find the words. When she'd been dating Levi, Chablis and Riesling knew. Neither one was living in town, so they didn't see what was going on, though they both visited, Chablis more than Riesling, but it was nice to have someone to talk to about her roller coaster of a ride with Levi. Things were different with that relationship.

Her problem with Levi was she didn't believe he was attentive enough with his child. He didn't see his kid enough and when his ex-wife remarried, he shrugged over the idea that she wanted to move to Texas, taking Levi's little girl with them.

And that's exactly what happened and that's when Zinny realized Levi wasn't the man for her at all. Their breakup wasn't even a blip on Levi's radar. He kissed her tenderly and told her he'd always remember her fondly.

Levi wasn't a bad guy; he was just married to his career. It's all he cared about. Everything else was white noise. But she'd cared deeply for Levi, and it had taken her some tears on the pillow before she'd been able to move past that relationship.

"I see," Chablis said. "Well, if you want to talk, I'll be around tomorrow." She kissed her cheek. "I can keep a secret."

Zinny knew without a doubt Chablis would never say a word to anyone.

But that wasn't the point. Zinny couldn't break Toby's trust. This wasn't about their sisterly bond. It was about her and Toby and what they meant to each other.

"I know," she said. Before she could say anything else, Dax came strolling out with a wicked smile.

"Hello, ladies." He looped his arm around Chablis. "Are you ready?"

"Hell, yes."

"Thanks for all your help with the ring and everything," Dax said. "I couldn't have pulled this off without you."

"I didn't know about any of this."

"No one but the boys did. I'm just lucky TJ didn't spill the beans." Dax nodded over his shoulder. "He and Toby are on their way out. But you should know, TJ did see his mom here."

"Shit. That's not good," Zinny said. "You two go have the night of your lives."

"Let's have lunch tomorrow," Chablis said. "I'll be at the winery first thing."

"Sounds like a plan." She kept her gaze locked on the front door, her thoughts with Toby and TJ. That had to be a tough conversation. She wondered if she should just leave.

The closer they got to the trial, the quieter and angrier TJ had become. Where he used to crack jokes and pick on Zinny, he sat in the front of her car either staring at his cell or looking out the window at the scenery.

The door to the arena opened and TJ and Toby appeared.

"You can go wait for me by my truck," Toby said. "I need to talk to Zinny before we take off."

"I need my backpack."

"You can get it from my car. I parked next to your dad." She handed TJ her keys. "You looked good on defense out there."

"Dax wants me to learn the position not just for power plays, but so I can fill in. He said he wants to use me a lot this year."

"That's good. Not a lot of freshmen get a lot of ice time." She wanted to ruffle his hair, but he was taller than her now and at fourteen, that probably wasn't a good idea. She watched him shuffle his way toward the back of the parking lot, his head down. "Dax said he saw Serena."

"I had to be the bigger person and tell him it was me who sent her away. He's pissed off and doesn't want to go out for pizza tonight. He wants to go home and sulk."

"It's good that you didn't lie to him, but did you explain why her showing up without even discussing it with you was—"

"Of course I did. I don't need a lesson on how to parent. I've been doing it for fourteen years." Toby raked a hand through his thick, dark hair. "I'm sorry, but obviously tonight is off."

"I understand." She did her best not to be offended by his words or his tone. He was dealing with a lot. "If you want to talk—"

"Can you meet me for coffee right after I drop him off at school in the morning?"

"Sure."

"Great. I'll see you at the Green Bean at seven." He moved past her without even touching her. He didn't say goodbye. Nothing.

She scurried off after him, but only because she needed her keys. Whatever was going on with him, she'd find out in the morning. Until then, she'd try not to think the worst.

This was about TJ.

Not her.

5

TOBY

Toby grabbed the fast-food tray and brought it to the table. He glanced at his watch.

He was going to be late.

Zinny didn't do well with that, but she'd understand. She'd have to.

"Here you go." Toby divided the food between him and his kid.

Last night Toby had given his son some room to be angry. He'd let TJ voice that frustration, mostly through silence, but now it was time to have a conversation about the realities.

"Since when do you let me be tardy for school?" TJ took the egg sandwich and opened it.

"We need to talk about what your mom did yesterday and why—"

"I get it, Dad. She's facing criminal charges. She did a bad thing and she's being punished." TJ snagged his orange juice and practically stabbed it with his straw. "But she didn't do anything to me, and I don't see what the harm would have been if she said hello."

"It's not that simple." Toby didn't want to get into the details of Serena's affair and who TJ's father was because that was information that he didn't want to get out. Not yet anyway. Maybe when TJ was an adult and mature enough to handle that kind of truth.

"Sure it is, unless you're keeping stuff from me."

"You're fourteen. And these are adult issues. Of course I am." Toby took a long sip of his coffee. There were things he could tell his son that didn't have to do with his heritage. "I want to protect you."

"If you're talking about all the things that Mom did when she was young, I've heard the rumors."

Toby's breath caught in his throat. "Could you please be specific?"

"Things she did to sabotage Dax's youth hockey career to make you look better. Everyone knows about those things."

"Where did you hear those stories?"

"Kids at school." TJ shrugged. "People at the rink started talking when Dax returned to be the head coach. I've heard them all."

"I see." TJ nodded.

"I know Mom does stupid things sometimes. But I don't understand why you sent her away. Why you threatened to call the cops on her."

"She told you that?" Shit. He should have known she'd pull a stunt like that.

"She might have mentioned it."

Toby couldn't lie. Not now. He'd look like an even bigger asshole. "For starters, your mom broke an agreement we had with the courts about visitation. And then there is the no parents rule at practice."

"But if you weren't going through a divorce, she'd be allowed to be sitting with you in the stands."

"No. She wouldn't," Toby said. "And that's not the point. These are the rules the judge came up with until after the trial. Once that is cleared up, there will be what is called a custody hearing. That will then decide—"

"Mom will be in jail."

"We don't know that." Toby wasn't sure how he felt about that concept. He wanted Serena to pay for what she'd done, but his kid was also paying the ultimate price. "Even so, I won't sugarcoat this. Let's say Mom doesn't go to prison. I want you to live with me when you're not living at school, and I'm going to fight for that. I do believe the mistakes your mother made are big enough to take away that right—that privilege."

"Don't I get a say?"

"You can express all your feelings to Doctor North as well as the judge when the time comes."

"You won't try to stop me from doing that?"

"No," Toby said, swallowing his heart. "I want you

to be honest, as I will be with you. And I don't believe living with your mom is a good idea."

TJ turned his head and swiped at his cheeks. "Why'd she do it?"

Oh. Wow. That was a loaded question and one Toby wasn't sure he could answer. "You're talking about why Mom and Grandma exposed Chablis' medical records?"

TJ nodded. "And I haven't seen or talked to Grandpa since it happened."

Toby had only spoken to John Weatherby once since the day of the arrest. John had a few choice words for everyone. He'd been pissed at his wife and daughter for disparaging the family name and he'd been really annoyed with Toby for not going to him so they could cover this up.

Since that day, John had gone to their house in Florida and hadn't come back. He was paying the legal bills, but outside of that, Toby thought they might never see the man again. Appearances meant everything to him.

"That's two very different questions." Toby wiped his face with his napkin and pushed his food aside. "As far as your Grandpa Weatherby goes, I don't know that he'll ever come back to Candlewood Falls and that has nothing to do with you, so don't ever think it does. When this dies down, I'll reach out to him and maybe we can take a trip to Florida."

"Without Mom?"

"Yes," Toby admitted. "You will have to accept that

your mother and I won't ever be getting back together. I can't forgive her for what she did to Dax and Chablis. That goes way below the belt."

"Mom told me she did all this for you. To make sure Dax didn't stay in town and someone else got the job. She said that you wanted Dax to leave and I think that's true."

Toby leaned back. "I'll admit that in the beginning I wasn't thrilled that Dax was going to be the head coach and I was concerned he'd take out the issues that he and I had on you, but we both know that's not the case."

TJ nodded.

"But I never wanted him to leave town. Or to not be with Chablis." Toby rolled his neck. "Look. My job is to protect you and right now, while we go through this trial with your mom and await that outcome, seeing her without the therapist present isn't possible."

"What if she doesn't go to jail?"

Toby let out a long breath. He'd given that a lot of thought. He still didn't want Serena around his son. He wanted full custody. If Serena was granted visitation, he was going to fight for it to be limited. But he didn't know how to tell his son that. "What do you want?" Toby knew it was a big risk asking TJ that, but the boy wasn't a baby. He was about to be a freshman in high school, with dreams of playing college hockey and more.

"I don't want this to follow me wherever I go. I

want to play hockey for CWF Prep. Maybe go play Juniors like you and Dax did and on to Division I," TJ said. "Dax told me that if things had gone differently for you, he was sure you would have made it in the NHL."

Toby's chest puffed out. It was nice to hear that Dax was filling his kids with that kind of admiration. Even if Toby wasn't sure if it was true. "I was the happiest in my hockey career when I played college at Boston University. It was a lot of fun. And honestly, I wouldn't trade being your dad for anything."

TJ cracked a smile.

It was something.

"I'm sorry that you're having to deal with some real grown-up stuff when all you should be doing is getting ready to enjoy your summer before high school," Toby said. "But this is our life right now and I need you to understand that the decisions I'm making are what I believe are best for us. I'm not doing it to punish you. But I do want to shelter you from as much hurt as possible."

"That's what Zinny says." TJ sucked down the last of his orange juice. "Is she picking me up today?"

"I've got meetings every day through the rest of the school year, so she's agreed to be your ride from school to the rink. I'll meet you there as soon as I can. If for some reason she can't, Dax said he could swing by."

TJ cringed. "Kids already think I'm his favorite."

"Talk to him about how that makes you feel."

"It's good and bad. I mean, who doesn't want to be in the coach's good graces, but I don't feel like I deserve it. I mean, I'm on third line and second power play line. It's not like I'm the best kid out there or anything."

"Wait. What? He picked the—"

"Oh, crap. I'm not supposed to tell anyone that."

"I'm sure I'll find out today at the coaches-manager meeting," Toby said. "But that's amazing. Third line will see a lot of ice."

"It beats the fourth line or worse, sitting in the stands. I feel bad for those kids. I'm not sure I'd want to be on the team."

"Maybe they just want to be a part of something and this is how they can do that."

"I hadn't thought about it that way."

Toby glanced at his watch.

Seven fifteen.

Shit. He was really going to be late. "We better get going. I'm going to have to sign you in."

"My first class is gym. No biggie," TJ said. "Dad?"

"What?"

"Do you like Zinny or something?"

Toby gripped the tray. He stood at the edge of the table and stared at his son. "Of course I like her. She's a good family friend. She's been your babysitter since you were a toddler and she's been a lifesaver through all this with just driving you around, especially since Grandma can't drive anymore." His heart dropped to the pit of his stomach. Maybe his kid didn't like having Zinny around. "Do you not want her picking you up and taking you places? Is that why you're asking?"

TJ shook her head. "No. She's cool. But Mom doesn't like her. She thinks since she's not in jail, she should be doing it."

Shit. This was not an easy discussion to have. "I'm sorry, buddy, but that's not going to happen. As long as you're happy with Zinny, then I am too."

"Yeah, well, you act all funny around her."

"Oh really. What does that mean?" Toby dumped the trash in the garbage. He opened the door, strolled outside, and found his key fob, unlocking his truck, trying to act nonchalant.

"It's as if you want to date her or something." TJ tossed his backpack in the back seat of the car. "And she's always smiling at you with her eyes. It's weird."

"How does someone smile with their eyes?" Toby climbed behind the steering wheel and fired up the engine.

"It doesn't matter." TJ exhaled. "Do you like her? And I promise, I won't tell Mom if you're worried about that. I swear."

Well, there was no getting out of this one. "It's complicated." But he had no idea how to answer it either. He couldn't tell his kid the truth, especially when last night he was ready to break up with Zinny.

Though he'd changed his mind a dozen times since then.

His mind and his heart were not in sync.

"Because she's younger?" TJ asked.

"That only scratches the surface." Toby backed out of the parking spot and headed toward the middle school. "There are—"

"I know about Mom's affair," TJ blurted out. "I have for a while."

"Excuse me?" Toby glanced at his son and nearly took out a telephone pole in the process. He pulled off to the side of the road. "What did you just say?"

"I know that Mom left because of another man. I met him."

Toby curled his fingers around the wheel until his knuckles turned white. He inhaled slowly through his nose and let it out through his mouth. He did this ten times. His wrath could not come out toward TJ. This was not his son's fault. TJ had nothing to do with Serena and Brooks and their affair.

Only, Brooks was TJ's biological father.

If Brooks wanted to stake a claim, he could. It didn't mean he'd get custody or even visitation, but it would fuck up TJ's life and make for an ugly court battle.

What the fuck was Serena thinking?

Certainly not about their son.

"When did you meet this man?" Toby asked as calmly as possible.

TJ swiped his eyes. "The first time was a year ago. He came to one of my games when you were out of town. I didn't know at the time, but I put it together pretty quickly. I'm not stupid."

"I know you're not, son." Toby reached out and took TJ's hand. "When was the second time?"

"After Mom moved out. We all went out to dinner. He said he was impressed with my hockey skills and that he was going to be taking over Dax's job." TJ's gaze dropped to his lap. "Mom wanted me to keep my eyes and ears open at the rink. She wanted me to report back to her if I heard anything about Dax or Chablis. But I swear, I never did hear anything or tell them anything."

"I know." Toby squeezed his son's hand. "I'm sorry you were put in that position."

"Mom told me that you were trying to take me from her and that she needed me to find stuff on you. Anything at all. This was so her, me, and Brooks could finally be a family."

Toby wanted to ask his son if Serena was still asking him to do these things, but that wouldn't be good parenting and he'd be stooping to her level. He was better than that. But he also had to protect himself. And TJ. "No one, including Mom, should be putting you in that kind of position, and I want you to feel comfortable telling your therapist these things."

TJ shrugged. "Mom's going to be mad I told you."

"These are adult situations that you shouldn't have to be dealing with. I don't want you to worry about any of it. However, if Mom starts on this kind of thing, I want you to tell her to stop. If she threatens you or makes you uncomfortable, you call or text me. Or your therapist. Or the social worker. You have her number. We'll all handle it from there."

"Yes, sir." TJ fiddled with his fingernail.

"Is something else bothering you?"

TJ made eye contact. "It's okay with me if you want Zinny to be your girlfriend."

Toby smiled. "I'll keep that in mind for when this trial is over."

Zinny

Zinny took her strawberry drink loaded with extra sugar and caffeine along with her chocolate-covered croissant and made her way to the outdoor patio where she took a seat and waited. She texted Toby, letting him know where she had planted her butt.

She stared at the screen, but no bubbles popped up.

Okay. He could be driving or sitting at the front of the school, chatting with his son.

It was ten to seven.

She was early.

She set her phone to the side and sipped her drink, staring off into the crowd. Sam Wilde stepped from the main cafe. He smiled and waved.

She returned the favor.

"Hey, you," he said as he approached. "How have you been? I hear you're working at the winery these days and might even go full-time."

"I gave my notice to my job, but they need me to train the new person who doesn't start for another week, so for the next month, I'm doing double duty."

"That's amazing. I honestly never thought I'd see the day you'd go to work for your parents." He waved at the seat. "Do you mind? There isn't a free table anywhere."

She opened her mouth to say she was meeting someone, but she couldn't say it was Toby. It didn't matter that she and Toby were seen together all the time because when that happened, TJ was with them.

"Oh. Are you meeting someone? I'll leave as soon as they get here. I just wanted a few moments to eat my muffin in peace before I head back to the orchard."

"Sure." She nodded. "How's Faith?"

"Oh. She's great. You should go see her for a reading."

Zinny waved her hands. "Oh no, thank you. That stuff isn't for me. But I heard she predicted Eliza Jane is having a girl."

"She sure did." Sam leaned in. "I bet she's right too." He winked.

She laughed. Sam always had the ability to lighten the mood, at least where Zinny was concerned.

Everyone called him a nerd. Or science boy. Or picked on him because he was different.

But to Zinny, he would always be sweet Sam. He was a couple years older and while he never paid her much attention in the romantic department when she had a huge crush on him, he always noticed her as a smart person with something to offer any discussion.

He never once discounted her opinions. As a matter of fact, he always encouraged her to speak her mind. She would always be grateful to him for that.

"Come on, don't you want to know—"

She held up her hands. "No. I don't test fate."

Sam laughed. "Well, you know where to find her if you change your mind."

"I won't, but thanks."

Sam reached across the table and pressed his hand over hers. "What's wrong? You don't seem your usual spunky self."

Leave it to Sam Wilde of all people to home in on her emotions.

"I'm just dealing with a lot of stuff right now."

"Does it have anything to do with Toby?"

"What do you mean?" She ran her hands up and down her jeans. She tried not to scrunch her nose because that would give way too much away and that was the last thing she wanted to do.

Not that Sam would ever give away any of her secrets. Again, he was a couple of years older and they weren't the best of friends growing up, but they had shared a common familiarity—they'd both been a bit of the black sheep of their families. Not in a bad way. But she and her twin brothers had been very different from their older siblings. Sam was quite different from the rest of the Wilde family. He was a nerd. A bookworm. A *Bill Nye the Science Guy* kind of man. When some other people implied that, they might have meant it in a mean way. Especially back in the day.

But when Zinny said it, she meant it with love and admiration.

She'd been a bit of a geek. Though her thing was math, not science.

The point was she preferred being smart over being popular, much like Sam. That concept brought her much grief growing up.

But not as much as being Weezer River's daughter.

"I know you have been spending a lot of time with him and his son. Not to mention your dad took on his divorce." Sam leaned back and raised his palms. "No one is gossiping about it, well, not that much if that's what you're worried about."

"Who's talking about it and what are they saying?" Zinny leaned closer, keeping her voice as calm and quiet as she could, which was a hard thing for her to do. It took a lot of restraint on her part.

"The town is rooting for Toby. I know that sounds mean in a way, but most people want to see him and TJ happy, and Serena brings Toby down and she's not the greatest mother."

Zinny wasn't going to argue those points, but she wasn't going to say them out loud to anyone other than her immediate family and Toby.

"No one liked what Serena tried to do to Chablis."

"Unfortunately, her arrest made headlines and now everyone knows what Chablis and Dax went through." Zinny resented how some people in this town judged her sister for the choice she made, especially in today's climate. It sucked that in so many states it was no longer a woman's choice to have an abortion.

But at least Chablis had been able to make the decision that had been right for her and Dax all those years ago. She held her head high and didn't care what others thought. Zinny admired her sister and Dax for that.

"I can't imagine having something like that out there for the world to examine, but also poor TJ. His world has to be upside down."

"It is. That's why I offered to help out."

"You're a good person, Zinfandel. I'm sure Toby appreciates all that you do."

Quickly, she lifted her cell. No texts from Toby and it was seven fifteen. He was never late for work. He could run late for other things, but he was a stickler for TJ being at school on time and that was fifteen minutes ago.

The school was ten minutes away.

"Thanks, Sam."

Sam finished his muffin and crumpled up his

napkin. "Well, I best be getting along. Don't be a stranger."

"See you later."

She wiggled her fingers and smiled. As soon as he was gone, she snagged her cell.

Still nothing. She sighed. Scrolling through her emails, she read a couple business ones. She couldn't wait until her second job was over and she could focus on working for the family business.

"Well, well, well," a familiar female voice said. "What do we have here?"

The contents of Zinny's stomach gurgled to the back of her throat, leaving a nasty taste in her mouth. She glanced up. "Serena," she managed between a tight jaw. "Can I help you?"

Serena made herself comfortable. She took a long sip of her coffee and lifted her sunglasses on top of her head.

The woman had a lot of nerve.

"You can," Serena said. "Next time you're with my boy, I want to see him. And you're not going to deprive me of my kid."

"We are not having this conversation." Zinny waved her hand across the table. "If you don't mind. I'm waiting for someone."

"I do mind." Serena folded her arms. "You don't have the right to keep me from my child."

"I'm not," Zinny said. "You did that all on your own." She dared to smile, sarcastically, of course.

Serena tilted her head and returned the expression. "You really are your mother's daughter."

"I take that as the highest compliment."

"You would," Serena mumbled, leaning forward, folding her hands on the table. "Either contact me when you pick up my son, or you'll be sorry."

"You don't scare me."

"I should because like your sister, I'm sure you have a skeleton in your closet, and if you don't make arrangements for me to see TJ, I'll find it and expose it."

"Good luck with that."

Serena stood, inching closer. "You don't want to make an enemy of me." She tapped the table with her knuckles. "I expect to hear from you this week."

Serena could have that expectation all she wanted, but it wasn't going to happen. There was only one secret that Zinny had and eventually it would either come out or it would end. Either way, she wasn't that concerned about it, with the exception of how TJ would handle the news because one thing she understood was that if he wasn't on board, it was over.

It was that simple.

Zinny waited for Serena to disappear before glancing at her phone.

Seven thirty.

Toby was half an hour late and no message.

She tapped his contact information. Her finger hovered over the green call button. Maybe he got called to work for an early meeting. Maybe he had to go into the school.

Or maybe he stood her up.

Ugh. She didn't like games and she wasn't going to play them.

Zinny: *Not sure what happened, but I have to get back to the winery. Text me when you can.*

With that, she stood and made a beeline for her vehicle, which she'd parked in the back lot.

"Zinny, wait up," Toby called.

She froze, standing by the hood of her car. Her heart hammered in her chest. She turned. "I just sent you a text."

He jogged across the pavement. "I'm so sorry I was so late. It couldn't be helped."

"I've got to get to the winery. My mom is on my ass to finish inventory by tonight."

He reached out and squeezed her arm. "We need to talk."

"About?" She folded her arms and tapped her toe.

"Don't be mad."

She arched a brow. "You could have texted. Or called."

"TJ was having a moment. He needed my full attention."

How the hell was she supposed to argue with that? Or be upset with him when he was doing the right thing?

She couldn't.

She dropped her hands to her thighs. "It's fine," she said. "But unless you drop TJ off at your mom's, when are we going to talk?"

"He's spending the night at CWF Prep for an incoming student event next Sunday so he can shadow one of the hockey players on Monday for classes."

"Isn't that following Monday when the trial dates are set?"

"Yup," Toby said. "So, if you can, I'll need you to pick him up from CWF Prep that day as well."

"I can do that."

He glanced over his shoulder before leaning in.

She pressed her hand on the center of his chest and pushed gently.

"Hey. Why'd you do that? I was just going to give you a quick kiss. No one is looking."

"Serena was at the coffee shop a little bit ago. If she's still lurking, there's no reason to give her ammunition."

He frowned. "I can't wait until this is over and we don't have to hide our relationship."

"I look forward to that as well." She pulled open the door.

"Before you leave, I owe you an apology."

"For what?"

"I was an asshole yesterday after Serena showed up at the rink and I'm sorry about the way I treated you. That was wrong. You deserve better."

Her lips tugged upward. "Thank you for that."

"I'll see you at the rink?"

"I can't stay this afternoon," she said. "But if you and TJ want to do pizza after practice, call me. If I'm not still knee-deep in counting wine bottles, maybe we can go grab a bite."

"I'd like that and I'm going to kiss you on the cheek. No one can fault me for that." He leaned in and let his lips linger on her skin for a long moment.

She inhaled sharply, enjoying every second. "Have a good day." She slipped behind the steering wheel. The next few months were going to be hard. She understood that and signed up for it because she was falling hard for Toby.

And his son.

6

CARTER

Carter sat on the back porch of the main house and wrapped his arm around Weezer. He stared out into the vineyard, watching his youngest child in a romantic lip-lock with Toby.

On the one hand, he was happy for Zinny because he'd seen a real change in his daughter. A calmness that he hadn't seen in her before. It was as if she were settling into her life with grace and ease. She enjoyed working at the winery. Thrived actually. It was incredible to watch her bond with her mother and older siblings.

Zinny had told him from a very young age that she knew her older siblings would return. She sensed that one day they'd all be working together.

Carter thought Zinny had been made of unicorns, rainbows, and red hair. She'd been the kind of kid who didn't believe in being negative. If someone told her she couldn't do something, she found a way to make it happen.

One of the reasons Carter—and Weezer—tried never to tell that child no.

"You have to admit they make for a cute couple," Weezer said with a light tone.

"I'm pleading the fifth on that." Carter didn't want to be a downer in this situation. He wanted to always be the one who supported his children, even if he didn't totally agree.

Though he didn't disagree. Zinny had always had a thing for older men. It was fitting since even though she bounced around like the Energizer Bunny with the attitude of her generation, she still had an old soul where romance was concerned.

And she was a little old-fashioned as well, even if she didn't want to admit it.

"They're good for each other. They really are." Weezer rested her hand on his thigh. "Remind me why TJ isn't here?"

"He's spending the night at CWF Prep." Carter kept his eyes on Toby and Zinny as they strolled through the vineyard arm in arm, Zinny gazing up at Toby, and he admired her as if she were the only person on this earth. "Some shadowing for next year so he can get the layout of the land. I remember when Dax did it. Malbec was a tad jealous. He thought it was so cool that one of his best friends was going to be living away from home."

Malbec and Eliza Jane sat at the picnic table with Trey, Riesling, Dax, and Chablis.

One more wedding to plan. It would be family only and in this very backyard, but it would be spectacular.

And there were two more grandchildren on the way.

Poor Eliza Jane was so uncomfortable he hoped she had that baby any day. Riesling wasn't due for a couple more months and she'd been down this road before. She glowed in her happiness because this time around, she had a man who truly loved her, and Carter and Weezer got to be by her side every step of the way.

Merlot and the twins, Noir and Nebbiolo, tossed a frisbee around the yard with Riesling's daughter, Ashling.

All his children in one place.

It made his eyes burn.

But he wouldn't cry.

He'd been dreaming of this day for years. Sure, they'd had holidays together even when Malbec lived in California and Chablis was fighting fires a few towns over and Riesling was barely speaking to them. Not to mention Merlot was doing his own thing an hour away.

But to have this every Sunday made his heart sing, especially now that he was back where he belonged.

"You haven't said anything to Zinny—or Toby— have you?" Weezer asked.

"That we know they're sneaking around? No," Carter said. "I suspect that Toby might not want his son to know yet. Or maybe he doesn't want to do anything that might hurt his custody case after the trial is over."

"And he thinks being with *our* daughter could possibly mean that he's not a good father or something, does he?"

Carter squeezed Weezer's shoulder. "The divorce won't be official for another week. He's got a teenaged boy. He's playing it smart."

"I just hope he's not using her," Weezer said. "I get he hasn't been able to officially end his marriage, but Serena cheated on him and he has the right to move forward, but I don't want Zinny to be a rebound."

"You just said they made for a sweet couple." Carter laughed.

"I don't want to see Zinny get her heart broken. She's got a sensitive soul and of all the men she's been with, she's fallen for him the hardest."

Carter didn't disagree with the last part of that statement, but he refused to believe that Toby would ever intentionally hurt Zinny. Sure, he'd made a lot of mistakes in his life. He'd done some shitty things in his past, but he'd always done right by his family. Ever since Toby had come to Carter asking him to draw up the adoption papers, Toby had been a good father. And when the shit hit the fan with Serena, Toby had done the best he could to make sure he protected his son, while also making sure his wife paid for what she did.

He didn't have to do that. He could have played that a dozen other ways, but Toby had come to Carter, scared and confused. He couldn't let Serena get away with what she'd done to Chablis, but at the same time, he wanted to keep his son safe. He wanted to make sure TJ knew he was loved and cared for while sending a message to Serena that she couldn't manipulate him or their son anymore.

"First, I don't think Toby is using Zinny. Second, she's a grown woman. We have to let her make her own choices, even if we don't like them."

"Are you saying you really don't approve of Toby just because he's older?"

"She's twenty-four. She's college-educated and has been living on her own, paying her own bills since she was twenty-one," Carter said. "She has your tenacity and both our work ethics. She's more of an adult than most of our children were at that age and certainly more than the twins combined." Carter sighed.

Weezer laughed. "I've almost lost hope for those two."

"I haven't. Nothing like the love of a good woman to change that." He lifted Weezer's hand and kissed it.

"Yeah, but they have to find a couple of those to put up with them."

Carter had no doubt that someday, the twins would find their forever person. Just like Merlot would find his.

And just like Zinny might have found hers in Toby. He nearly choked on that thought. Not that he didn't want his baby girl to find the right man. He absolutely did. And Toby was a stand-up guy. At least he'd turned out to be one. It was just a big pill to swallow that his little girl—the youngest child—might have found *the one.*

He rubbed the back of his neck. He hated that he had reservations about this union before he was even given the chance to be the mean old dad with a shotgun. Sadly, that's not what this couple was going to need, and Toby's son would need a world of support. His mother could be going to jail. Or at the very least, she would be on probation with a felony charge. That would change her life forever.

Weezer pinched his side.

"Hey. That hurt."

"You're being way too serious. That's usually me in this situation."

"It takes a special person to date one of our children knowing how we are," Carter said.

"But our bark is worse than our bite."

"Most people don't honestly know that about us, and Toby has only seen us through the eyes of Serena and her family. That has never been good because even though we didn't approve of Dax when he was a teenager, we treated him a million times better than we ever treated Serena and her family."

"I've never liked her mother. Or her grandmother. If anyone ever thought I was a gossip. Good Lord. They make Clarise Chambers seem like a normal person."

"That could never happen," Carter said. "Oh, my.

Look." Carter pointed to Toby and Zinny sharing a tender kiss under the sunset. "I don't think I can deal with giving away another daughter. Especially my baby."

"Just think, it will be the last girl. You will just have boys left."

"That's not really making me feel any better." Carter wished he could peel his gaze away from the couple stealing a kiss at the edge of the vineyard.

But he couldn't.

It reminded him of when he'd fallen in love with Weezer.

"Do you think they know we can see them?" he asked.

"Yes," Weezer said. "I feel like they've been easing into telling us all afternoon, but didn't know how."

"I guess they just did."

"Will this change you taking his case?"

"Absolutely not," Carter said. "He doesn't want to be married and his divorce will be easy."

"What about custody?"

"That will all be dependent on how this criminal case turns out. If Serena gets time, Toby will get full custody, no questions asked. If not, that's a different story. But I will go to bat for him. He's a good dad. I think that shows."

"If Zinny stays with him, she's taking on being a stepmom to a teenager."

"I'm pretty sure she's aware of that." Carter chuckled. It wasn't really funny, but it was the way in which he and his wife went back and forth. Sundays had always been his favorite day. Even when his family had been splintered and only a few of his children had come back to the vineyard.

He loved these moments sitting on the porch with the love of his life and whoever of his children were around. He had one grandchild and two more on the way. His family was constantly growing and he couldn't be happier.

Especially now that he'd moved back home after years of being separated from the only woman he'd ever loved.

The only woman he'd ever been with.

Weezer made his heart beat a little faster and he couldn't ever imagine being with anyone else.

Ever.

"Here they come," Weezer whispered as if he couldn't see them strolling across the front yard hand in hand. "How do we handle this?"

"With love and kindness," Carter said. "And very little sarcasm and teasing."

Toby

"I can't believe we're doing this." Toby tried to pull his hand away, but Zinny wouldn't let him. "I'm pretty sure your entire family just saw me shove my tongue down your throat."

"Ew. That is not the way I'd like that kiss to be described."

Toby laughed. It wasn't a funny one. More of a nervous, high-pitched cackle. "Do you think your mom has her famous shotgun behind that sofa she and your dad are sitting on?"

"Probably," Zinny said with a serious tone. "We're lucky they haven't used you for target practice yet."

"You're not helping."

"Because you're being ridiculous."

"Am I?" Toby inhaled sharply. The intense grape aroma filled his nostrils. He hadn't been this nervous when he went home to tell his mother that he was marrying Serena and adopting her baby.

His mom hadn't appreciated Serena like his dad had. Until TJ had turned maybe six or seven, his mother had tolerated Serena. But then Serena turned into her old self when it came to TJ and hockey. It was like watching a train drive back to his youth, only he stood on the outside and watched his wife behave much like his dad had.

And then Toby fell in line.

When he thought about some of the things he'd said to fellow coaches or other parents, he cringed. He was truly grateful he had a second chance at being a good hockey parent and with Zinny, a good boyfriend.

"My folks already like you," Zinny said. "My dad wouldn't take on your case or help Levi if—"

"That's another thing." Toby stopped dead in his tracks. "Why didn't you tell me you used to date Levi?"

"Because its none of your business and my dad doesn't know."

Toby cocked a brow. "Are you sure about that?"

"Well, no. But I never told him. Nor did Levi," Zinny said.

"Do you have a thing for older men?" Not that it mattered, but Toby was curious now.

"Every man I've been involved with has been older." Zinny palmed his cheek. "It all started with Sam Wilde."

"You dated Science Boy?"

Zinny rolled her eyes. "No. And don't call him that. I've always hated it when Malbec and Dax did that. He was a nice boy who happened to be really smart and into science when we were kids. And he's not that much older than me, but he was my first official crush."

"What do you think of him now?"

She fanned herself. "He's sexy."

"Oh, my God. My girlfriend has the hots for nerdy Sam Wilde." He shook his head. "I could understand if it was his cousin, Brad. Even I might get all hot and bothered under the collar for him. But Sam? Are you yanking my chain?"

"Nope. I really do think Sam is adorable. Not in the conventional way, but there's something about him that I've always admired. He's sweet and kind and cute." She leaned in and pressed her mouth gently over Toby's in a slow, tender kiss. "But you don't have to worry. He hasn't done it for me since the tenth grade." She tugged at his hand. "Come on. Let's get this conversation over with so we can at least be open about our relationship with my family."

"I knew there was something going on," Chablis said as they walked by. She and Dax sat at the picnic table with Malbec, Eliza Jane, Trey, and Riesling.

Just what Toby needed.

Half the family in one shot.

Wonderful.

"I didn't know," Trey said. "I'm always the last to know anything in this family."

"That's because we're outlaws." Eliza Jane leaned back against Malbec and rubbed her big belly. "But I suspected."

"That's because Chablis and I were talking about it the other day," Malbec said. "And you overheard."

"I'm glad Toby and I gave you all something to gossip about." Zinny squeezed his hand.

Tight.

It was so hard he thought his fingers turned white.

Of course, he wondered if his face had drained of all the blood that was supposed to be circulating through his body.

"How long has this been a thing?" Dax asked.

"Not that long," Toby admitted, feeling like he needed to add to the conversation. He'd gone through grade school with Dax and Malbec. If he had gone to regular school, he would have graduated with Malbec. They were all the same age. And Chablis and Riesling weren't all that far behind.

Merlot came jogging over with the twins.

Shit.

This was too much.

"You dog." Merlot punched his shoulder. "You and my baby sister, eh?"

"You're not from Canada." Toby raked a hand through his hair. "And yeah. Me and Zinny. What of it?" He puffed out his chest and then wished he hadn't when he remembered that Merlot used to be a parole officer and he probably still carried a gun.

Not a smart move.

"Why couldn't TJ come?" Ashling climbed up on the picnic table bench and plopped herself between Riesling and Trey. "I like playing with him. He's nice to me."

"I'm glad," Toby said. "But he's at a school function tonight." Toby tapped the center of his chest. It was June. In a couple of weeks, his kid would be moving into the dorms for the summer hockey program. And at the end of August, he'd be living there for the school year.

That was going to be hard.

"Will he be here next Sunday for our family dinner?" Ashling asked.

Toby swallowed.

Everyone stared, waiting for an answer.

But Toby was stuck on the word family and the fact that this was an every weekend thing.

"I think that's going to be up to Grandma and Grandpa," Trey said, breaking the silence.

"Do you think they will come down here and talk to us?" Toby didn't dare glance over his shoulder in fear there might be a loaded shotgun pointed in his direction. In reality, he knew that wasn't the case. Even the Weezer wasn't that barbaric. But she could be damn scary at times.

So could Carter.

"No. They will make you go to them," Dax said. "They are going to act as though they hate you and be all serious, but trust me, they are big teddy bears."

"They won't be that hard on you." Chablis smacked Dax's shoulder.

"Oh yes, they will." Nebbiolo said. "You all have to remember that it was so different for me, Noir, and Zinny. It's like we were raised by two different sets of parents. And Zinny truly is Dad's favorite."

"No. I am," Riesling said, tossing her hair back and laughing.

"Not even close," Chablis said. "Nebbiolo is right. Zinny is not only the youngest, but she's a girl and Dad has always had a soft spot for her. Toby is Malbec's age and while that's not really a big deal, I'm sure all Dad can think about is the time he caught Malbec making out with Rachel while Zinny was crawling around the vineyard eating our finest grapes during harvest."

"She was lost for an hour," Riesling said. "We had the cops out here and everything."

"Dad was so pissed," Merlot said. "He threatened to stop paying for college."

"I remember that." Dax shook his head. "Zinny had grapes stuffed in her diaper and could barely even walk when everyone found her."

Zinny groaned. "I was three. It wasn't a diaper. I had them in my dress. And for the record, I wasn't lost. I knew exactly where I was."

"Didn't that make headline news? Wasn't there a picture?" Toby asked.

"Yes. There was," Reisling said. "She was covered in grapes. We all believe this is why she loves sugar so much."

"You all can stop talking like I'm not even here," Zinny said.

"Aw. Sorry, sweetheart." Toby wrapped his arm around her and kissed her temple.

"You two should probably go talk to Mom and Dad. They look like they are getting restless," Malbec said.

Toby blinked. It wasn't so much that he was afraid of Weezer and Carter—though that was part of it—but this made everything so real. When Serena moved out in April, he hadn't given any thought to ever dating.

His life had become about protecting his son. About being a good father.

Zinny had played a huge role in doing that simply because she was there, always willing to help.

"Let's do this." He turned and immediately wanted to crawl under a rock.

Weezer snuggled up next to Carter on the outdoor sofa on the back porch of the house. Carter had his arm around Weezer.

Neither one smiled.

They just sat there.

Staring.

At Toby.

"Relax," Zinny said, but not with her normal level of confidence. "We're not going to die or anything."

He chuckled. "But I might lose my right arm."

"More likely your left."

"You're really not funny, Zinny."

"At least all of your siblings aren't here to watch this," she whispered.

He wasn't about to point out that he didn't have any as they took the steps slowly, one at a time.

"You two look awfully cozy," Carter said with a dark tone. He didn't move an inch, except his eyes as they shifted with every step that Toby and Zinny took. "Why don't you pull up *separate* chairs."

That was a statement and Toby did exactly that. He adjusted one for Zinny and then pulled one in for himself.

Carter motioned to the table behind them. "Before you sit down, why don't you pour us all some wine."

"Yes, sir." Toby took the two half-empty glasses that were in front of Carter and Weezer and started with those, hoping his hands didn't shake.

He remembered when he'd asked John Weatherby if he could marry Serena. He'd been insanely nervous, but all John had to say was good luck with that one and I'm cutting her allowance in half. John then grabbed a drink, but only for himself, and walked away.

John was a tough nut.

Carter not so much.

But Toby cared about what Carter thought. His opinion on just about everything mattered to him. Carter was well respected in town. Everyone loved him. Even those who didn't like Weezer enjoyed being around Carter.

It was an interesting pairing, and if you looked at them separately, you wouldn't understand.

Seeing them together, it made perfect sense.

Toby set the first two glasses down before preparing two for him and Zinny.

"Are you ready for tomorrow?" Carter asked as if this were going to be a discussion about anything other than his and Zinny's relationship.

"I'm ready to get this over with." Toby handed Zinny her flute. He smiled.

She'd moved her seat a little closer.

Carter cleared his throat.

"But I also know tomorrow is just the beginning. The trial is where the real fun will begin," Toby said.

"You do know Levi will make one last offer for this to be settled without going to trial." Carter lifted his feet and placed them on the table, crossing his ankles.

Toby nodded. "I have mixed feelings about that."

Carter raised his glass and swirled, watching the red liquid hug the sides of the glass. "I do as well. Going to trial is always a crapshoot and we want a conviction."

"Do you think she believes she'll be found not guilty and actually be given custody of TJ?" Zinny asked.

"She wouldn't be playing this card if she didn't," Carter said. "But what concerns me is what her lawyer might believe. Anna Delvecy is a smart woman. If she believes she can win, she'll go hard. But if she has reservations, she'll push her client to settle. Anna doesn't like to lose in court."

"Should I be concerned?" Toby asked. "And while I appreciate you taking on both my divorce and my custody case, why does Serena have more than one lawyer? It's confusing to me."

"Anna is an excellent criminal lawyer. It's all she does. She wouldn't touch a custody case if her life depended on it," Carter said. "While I am a jack of all trades, I prefer family law. I wouldn't say I specialize in it, since when it comes to the people in this town who I care about, I'll do what it takes for them, but family law is one of the reasons I wanted to become a lawyer."

"What do you know about her other lawyer? The one representing her in the custody hearing."

"One problem at a time," Carter said. "Let's focus on Anna first. I'll deal with Odette Moira when the custody case begins."

"I'm worried about tomorrow. So much of it is out of my control."

"I understand," Carter said. "I'll be in the court-room tomorrow. I've gone up against Anna a couple of times. I'm hoping I can get a good read on Serena and what she's intending on doing after the trial, but really, we can't lay out our strategy for custody until the end of this."

"I'm worried she'll file a motion or something for during trial. She's showed up at the rink once. She's calling and texting TJ when she's not supposed to be," Toby said.

"She even asked me to bring TJ to see her, but I ignored her," Zinny said.

"You didn't tell me that." Toby jerked his head and glared. "When did that happen? What exactly did she expect you to do?"

"About two weeks ago and it doesn't matter. I haven't heard from her since. It was all smoke and mirrors on her part." Zinny patted his leg.

"I don't like that woman coming anywhere near you." Weezer took a long sip of her beverage.

"Nor do I. And we have to be prepared for Serena and whatever she might try to pull out of her ass. She fights dirty. She always has." This was why Toby didn't want to make his relationship with Zinny public. However, she made a valid point that her father needed to know.

And perhaps Levi.

"We're well aware what she's capable of," Weezer said with real disgust laced in her words.

Toby didn't take it personally. He'd been with Serena on and off since they were fourteen. He'd been fed up with her by the time he'd turned seventeen and he spent five years away from her and he hadn't looked back. His life had finally been his own.

Away from the shadow of Dax.

Away from his parents and what they wanted for him.

And away from Serena and her antics.

However, a little over a year after he graduated, his mom had called, begging him to come home. His father was near death and wanted to make amends with his only son.

Sadly, that's not exactly what his dad wanted, but Toby was glad he'd made the effort. Besides, his mom needed him as she wasn't doing well with anything.

But then Serena came back to town.

There was always a part of Toby that wondered if his dad had anything to do with it, but Serena denied it.

That didn't mean shit.

Carter dropped his feet to the wood floorboards.

"We're just sorry that's it come down to this." He set his drink on the table and clasped his hands together. "Tomorrow should be quick and painless. Levi will read the charges. She'll plead not guilty again and the judge will set a date. I'm guessing it will be in maybe a week. Two tops since the discovery documents have all been shared and the list of witnesses is short. I also know this judge and she doesn't like things to sit in the balance. "

"I want it over with." Toby squeezed Zinny's hand. "I want my divorce to be final. And I want to keep full custody of TJ."

Carter grabbed his flute and took a hearty sip. "So, this is why we're sitting here right now. Because the two of you have something you're trying to tell us." He waved his hand in their direction. "Or show us."

"Yes, sir." Toby sat up a little taller. His heart jumped from the center of his chest to the top of his mouth and then dropped to the pit of his stomach like a brick. He opened his mouth, but had no idea what to say. "I care about Zinfandel."

"I don't doubt that," Carter said. "But it's going to be best if Zinny doesn't come to the courtroom during the trial, except for when she's called to testify."

"We've already discussed that. I'll be with TJ," Zinny said.

"We figured that was the best course of action since everyone is so used to seeing them together." Toby inhaled sharply and blew out a puff of air. "I didn't want to change things because I thought that might bring attention to Zinny, and then people might wonder why she all of a sudden wasn't helping out."

"That's a good point." Carter nodded. "But you need to be careful. People are going to judge the age difference."

"Right now, I only care about what you and Mrs. River think." Toby tried to ignore the pounding pulse between his ears.

Weezer laughed. "Since when do you call me that?"

"Another thing that should remain the same," Carter said. "Appearances matter. I've had my clients over before. And you and TJ have been here, so no one is going to bat an eyelash about this. But if you start calling Weezer Mrs. River, well, that's a red flag. Don't give people a reason to talk about you and I'd be saying that if you weren't just kissing my baby girl."

"Yes, sir," Toby said.

"Stop calling me sir." Carter shook his head. "When did this thing with the two of you start?"

"The last time TJ and Toby came for Sunday dinner." Zinny ran her thumb over the top of his hand. She turned and smiled.

Every single time she did that he wanted to fall right off his chair.

"So, this is very new," Weezer said.

"Is there anything about this relationship I need to know for the divorce or custody hearings?" Carter asked. "Anything that Serena might be able to use against you?"

"I don't think so," Toby said. "We haven't told anyone."

"What about TJ?" Carter asked.

"He doesn't know," Toby admitted. "But he's also not opposed."

"Really?" Zinny tilted her head. "How do you know that?"

"He basically gave me permission to take you out, but I just don't think it's a good idea for us to be doing that until this is over." Toby couldn't believe how good it felt to finally be having this discussion. It wasn't half as scary as he thought it was going to be.

"Hiding it isn't necessarily the right thing either because that could come off like you're ashamed," Carter said.

"I most certainly am not." Toby squared his shoulders.

"I didn't say you were." Carter set his glass down and stood. He made his way to the stairs and stuffed his hands in his pockets. "When Weezer and I divorced and I moved out, it was because she was holding on to this damning family secret. She was trying to protect me by keeping it from me when all it did was put a strain on our relationship and gave this town a lot to talk about."

Toby swallowed his breath. The last thing he wanted was to bring the spotlight more to himself, but especially to his son. He knew during the trial it would be impossible to avoid the attention, but eventually things would die down and the only thing people could say about him and Zinny was the age difference. "Are you suggesting we continue to hide our relationship?"

"I'm not sure. We might consider having you and Zinny ease into being seen in public alone together, especially if TJ is okay with the two of you dating," Carter said. "Or maybe we can start off with having Toby with us at the unveiling of our new wine. That's generally only a family affair. If he's here at Zinny's side when the press takes pictures, they will pose the question. We'll answer it. It should kill all the birds with one powerful stone."

"It will do more than that," Weezer said. "Because it will stop people from whispering and gossiping behind their backs. Or about how I must be taking the news and how enraged I could be. But instead, they will see with their own eyes I'm okay with it."

"No." Zinny shook her head. "It's too staged. It will all look phony. Like a photo op."

"Perhaps I should take Zinny on a proper date."

"But we can't be guaranteed the press will be there to see you," Weezer said.

"But if we go to a restaurant right in town, everyone will see us. They will start talking," Zinny said. "It would be better if we all went out. The four of us. I know that's not exactly what we want, but it will have the desired effect at least from the perspective that my family approves."

"Would your mom be up for a night out on the town?" Carter turned. "That's an even bigger statement and Zinny is right. It would be less staged."

"She'd love it. She doesn't get out much, especially since she can't drive anymore." Toby worried about his mom. He had no idea how loveless her marriage had been until his father had died, but her health had always been a struggle.

"How old is she?" Weezer asked.

"She's only sixty-three, but she has lupus and the last six years have been really hard on her." Toby polished off his wine.

"That's young." Carter nodded. "Why don't we set something up at the courthouse tomorrow?"

"Sounds like a plan." Toby rested his hand on Zinny's thigh and squeezed.

"But don't get too comfortable with your hands on my daughter," Carter said. "My shotgun is loaded and I'm not afraid to use it."

"Carter," Weezer said. "That's my line."

"I think this is my cue to quietly leave." Toby let out a slight laugh. He shifted his gaze between Zinny and her parents, hoping he'd read the situation properly.

He was greeted with blank stares.

He cleared his throat. "I think I need to get to know Trey a little better."

"He can't help you," Carter said. "We liked him

from the very beginning. You've been skating on thin ice since we met you." Carter smiled. "I've been waiting all afternoon to say that."

"O-M-G, Dad. That's so stupid." Zinny jumped to her feet. She stepped over Toby and wrapped her arms around her dad. "No picking on my boyfriend. I've never really brought one home, so be nice."

"That's because they're usually ten years or so older." Carter took Zinny into his arms. "Or one of them worked for me and you didn't want me to know."

"You knew about Kyle?" Zinny squinted.

Toby closed his eyes and counted to ten before opening them. He really didn't want to hear any of this, but he wasn't left with a choice.

Carter laughed. "I've known about them all, but I don't want to embarrass Toby any more than he already is."

"I appreciate the kindness," Toby said softly. "For someone who is a few years younger, she seems to have more dating experience than I do."

"As a father, I'm going to say that's working in your favor," Carter said. "Now, how about you help grill some food. I don't know about you, but I'm starving."

"Not to brag, but I'm good behind a grill." Toby stood and rested his hand on the small of Zinny's back. He dared to press his lips on her cheek. Even though he knew he would be facing some challenging times, he felt like for the first time in years, he had the chance at real happiness.

7

ZINNY

Zinny had been inside Toby's house a million times, and each time she had stepped inside since Serena had moved out, she felt more comfortable in it.

He'd bought this house ten years ago. She remembered the day. She'd been fourteen and TJ had been four. Serena had called Zinny asking if she could babysit for the whole weekend. Spend the night and everything. Serena was willing to pay top dollar. Even though Zinny couldn't stand Serena, she loved spending time with TJ and she needed the money.

Toby hadn't been thrilled by the amount of money Serena had promised, or the fact Serena hired Zinny to not only watch TJ, but to do most of the unpacking, but Zinny hadn't cared.

Money was money.

She set her purse on the table by the back door and

made her way into the family room. There wasn't a trace of Serena left in the house, but Zinny felt strange about spending the night. She certainly wasn't there to babysit. She was there as Toby's girlfriend. His lover. She would be sharing his bed.

That's where the cement brick landed in the pit of her stomach.

"Are you okay?" Toby leaned against the counter in the kitchen and folded his arms. "You've barely said a word since we left your parents'."

"I'm not a jealous person." She tucked her hair behind her ears and awkwardly took a seat at the table. She fiddled with the napkin holder. A long silence filled the air. She didn't know how to get this out. It seemed childish.

"Um. I'm not following," Toby said.

"You know I've stayed overnight here before." She glanced up, catching his gaze.

"That was very different," he said. "What's going on with you?"

She decided this was like ripping off a bandage. Only one way to do it. Fast. "The bed we are going to sleep in you shared with Serena."

"Oh. I see."

"Do you? Because I feel stupid."

He meandered in her direction with a wicked smile. He stood behind her and placed his hands on her shoulders, massaging gently. "Why?"

"Because you're divorcing her for starters, so I shouldn't feel that way."

"It's normal," he said. "Besides, if you think it will be fun for me to see Levi tomorrow, well, think again."

She glanced up. "That's kind of different. I wasn't married to him, nor did I ever live with him."

"Maybe," he said. "But that doesn't change that I will have a visceral reaction because you once had feelings for him, had a sexual relationship with him, and I know how you are. You don't do things half-assed. If you don't genuinely have a deep emotional tie to someone, you're not going to get involved with them."

Toby was right. If her feelings were lukewarm, she walked away, not bothering to even date the person. She probably missed out on some decent men, but she was a passionate person. She didn't want mundane in her personal life. She had enough of that when she was selling wine. If it wasn't her family brand, it was hard to get excited.

Whoever was going to be her man, she needed them to make her pulse jump out of her skin.

Toby did that and then some.

She also had to admit that Levi had been fun, while it lasted. He'd been great in bed, and he was an amazing lawyer. But the problem had always been that he wasn't necessarily the best dad.

And that meant something to Zinny.

"Well, you're not about to spend the night where Levi

did," she said. "For the record, the bed in the cottage on the winery is brand new. Other than me, you're the only person who has slept in it. The bed here, well—"

He leaned over and hushed her with a kiss. "I bought a new one when Serena moved out because I let her take ours."

"Oh. Well, that does help a little."

Toby lifted her from the chair. "Other than the fact I will always be grateful that I have TJ, I have no feelings for Serena left. She's bled me dry and I can't even feel sorry for her anymore. I only feel bad for our kid and how what she's done is going to affect his life."

"You're an excellent father." She palmed Toby's cheek. "You have done everything in your power to make sure TJ knows he's loved and cared for. You've also tried to keep his life the same. You've made sure he can still go to CWF Prep. You didn't take that job in New York to ensure his life wasn't uprooted. I know he appreciates that."

"He does." Toby smoothed his hands over her ass. "However, I didn't want to take that job anyway. I can't be that far from my mom."

"That's not really what Serena says."

He laughed. "I know. She's told a couple of different stories. One of them is that she forced me not to take it. That she gave me an ultimatum, which is laughable. The other one is that I didn't get that job, but I tell people I turned it down. That's kind of my favorite."

"You have never corrected anyone. Why?"

"I guess I don't see the point," he said.

"You sound like my mother." She wrapped her arms around his shoulders. "She's never felt the need to put right all the rumors that surround her or our family. Sometimes I think she gets off on the insanity of it."

"At this point in her life, she probably does." Toby brushed his lips across Zinny's cheek. "My mom has always admired Weezer and wished she could have been more like her in so many ways, but especially in not caring what others thought. That had always been a big problem with my dad and why he went after Dax so hard. Growing up, my dad always felt like he was in his big brother's shadow. He resented the hell out of it and that's probably why he only had one kid and why he struggled with me being second to Dax."

"How did you really feel about it?"

"I was a child. I wanted to please my dad, so I hated it. But when I looked back, I never actually minded it. If I could go back in time and change one thing about my life, it would be how I handled that, but then there would be a ripple effect and I wouldn't have TJ and I wouldn't be standing here with you."

"Aw. That's sweet, but it's pretty much in the bag that you're going to get laid tonight."

"Wait. You mean I don't have to work for it? I don't have to be all romantic and sweet and woo you?"

"I'm a sure thing. Unless you say something stupid between here, the bedroom, and the time we take off our clothes."

He grabbed her by the hand and tugged.

"Whoa. What are you doing?" Butterflies filled her gut in anticipation.

He paused at the bottom of the stairs. "Do I really have to explain my intentions? Or can I just start doing this?" He lifted the bottom of her shirt and yanked it over her head, letting it drop to the floor. His hands slid up the sides of her body, across her back, and quickly unhooked her bra.

She breathed slowly and methodically. Every time she'd been with him, she felt like she'd been stealing his time.

A quickie after he snuck into her cottage and then he'd rush out so he didn't get caught. It was always rushed, but passionate and playful. She loved that about Toby.

But tonight they had hours to be in each other's arms and she wanted some normalcy. Something that said they were a couple.

She reached behind her and reclasped her undergarment. She turned on her heel and slinked up the stairs, swinging her hips seductively. Pausing at the top, she glanced over her shoulder. "I think I want a bottle of champagne and some strawberries."

"I have both of those things." Toby planted his hands on his hips.

"I'll draw a bath while you get them."

He tilted his head. "I think someone wants to be wooed."

"Don't use that word." She laughed. "I've just always wanted to use that big tub of yours and sometimes a little seduction is necessary." She kicked up her leg and headed down the hallway. Never in her life had anyone made her heart thump so heavy.

She understood she didn't have a lot of experiences and if any of her siblings heard her say something like that out loud, they'd laugh in her face. The four older ones would all tell her she hadn't lived enough to know what real heartache was and maybe they were right.

Her life had been easy compared to theirs. She'd never had the rift with her parents that her older siblings had. She and the twins got along with everyone. They had decent relationships with all the brothers and sisters as well as their parents. She didn't feel slighted because her parents were divorced like Riesling and Merlot had. She hadn't resented her parents over secrets and lies like Malbec and Chablis because she'd been kept in the dark even more so than they had.

All she knew was that there was drama, but she wasn't part of it and she loved that fact.

Everyone thought she was just like her mother. That was true in the energy department. And maybe in the meddling department because she liked to fix things. To make things right.

But the one place she differed from her mom had been in the way she handled her relationships with either the media or the people of Candlewood Falls.

Her mother allowed people to think whatever they wanted. She didn't care if she was totally misunderstood.

Zinny hated that. She didn't like it when people got her wrong. She preferred if anyone was going to dislike her, they did so for the right reasons. The real reasons.

She wanted to correct them, but her mother always told her that it wasn't her place because why did it matter? Changing that narrative wasn't going to change if someone liked her or not, and Zinny couldn't argue with that philosophy, but she still couldn't stop herself from making sure the world saw Zinny the way she wanted to be seen.

She filled up the tub with hot water. She reached for the bottle of bubble bath and groaned.

Serena.

Zinny held the designer bottle in her hands and stared at it for a long moment. A plastic seal covered the top, so it hadn't been opened. That should make her feel better about using it, but a pinch of jealousy didn't go away and that pissed her off. She didn't understand it. There was no reason to be jealous of Serena. Toby had no love left for her and Zinny knew it. He would be forever connected to her because of TJ and Zinny could—her heart dropped like a ton of bricks.

She placed a hand over her stomach, understanding where the jealousy came from, finally. For weeks she hadn't been able to place why Serena had gotten under her skin. It wasn't because she was worried that Toby had feelings for Serena. Sure, Zinny hadn't wanted to sleep in a bed Toby shared with Serena.

What woman did?

But Zinny struggled to understand why that bothered her so much. She let her mind and soul believe her heart had become insecure when in reality, he had jumped somewhere else.

Serena had given Toby his son. The one thing Toby valued above all else, as it should be. Zinny knew that if Toby ever had to choose, he'd pick his son.

That didn't bother Zinny in the slightest.

But what did was the fact that Zinny wanted a family. She wanted a husband and she wanted that man to be Toby.

She couldn't deny the fact that she'd fallen in love with him if she tried. At least not to herself.

And she loved TJ with her entire being. She knew she would never take the place of his mother, even if Serena ended up in jail. But she wanted to be in TJ's life.

But Zinny wanted more.

She continued to hold the bubble bath bottle in her hands, staring at it. She wasn't jealous over the fact that either Serena had bought it or Toby had purchased it for her. That had nothing to do with Zinny's emotions.

However, Zinny wanted a child of her own someday. She wanted to feel what it was like to grow life in her belly. To share that experience with the man she loved.

She sighed as she tore open the bottle, dumping a fair amount of liquid into the water.

It bubbled immediately.

Shedding her clothing, she submerged herself into the hot water. At first, it prickled her skin, but she soon got used to it. She eased back and closed her eyes, blocking her mind from drifting off into what the future might hold.

She was only a month into this thing with Toby and there were so many uncertainties.

And too many conversations they hadn't had yet.

Right now, she simply needed to enjoy the moment.

"Looks like I need to catch up." His voice rolled off her ears like melting chocolate over ice cream.

She blinked.

He set a bowl of strawberries on the tray over the tub before pouring two glasses of champagne. He handed her one and set his on the tray. Quickly, he removed his clothing and joined her, sloshing the water. He clinked his glass against hers and smiled. "I've lived in this house for ten, almost eleven years and I've never once been in this tub."

"Are you serious?"

"I'm not even sure Serena really used it. We used to give TJ baths in it when he was little, but that was about it." He took a strawberry, which he'd taken the time to cut off the green parts and he plopped it in her mouth.

A lightness filled her insides. She took way too

much pleasure in the fact that this was the first time he'd used the tub this way. It seemed silly and childish, but it meant something to her in a way she could barely describe.

If they were to go the distance, she was going to have to accept he'd already been married, so she'd be a second.

He already had a kid.

He might not want to have another one.

Oh boy. That might be a deal breaker.

"What's going on with you tonight?" He reached out and ran his thumb across her cheek. "Is your mind thinking about tomorrow already?"

"It's hard not to."

"But tomorrow means nothing other than when the trial begins."

"I know." She sipped her champagne, wanting it to go right to her head. She hated that she wasn't being completely truthful with Toby. But it was too soon and there were too many unknowns for her to go down that road yet.

"Sweetheart, something else is bothering you. Please tell me what it is."

Her breath got caught in the center of her chest. It was as if her heart captured it and was holding it hostage until she bared her soul. But that would overload and he'd jump from this bath and run.

Hell, she felt like hiding under the bubbles, it was too much.

But she'd made him a promise she'd always be open.

That included this.

"I care about you." Her throat felt like she'd swallowed an entire bottle of glue. Not the liquid kind. But that thick goopy, syrupy kind that began to adhere the moment it had been applied to anything.

He traced his index finger across her lips. "I know. The feeling is mutual."

"I care about TJ."

He took both their glasses and set them on the floor. "You're telling me things I know, I see, and I feel." He tucked a few strands of hair that had fallen from her ponytail behind her ears. "There's more to what's going on in that pretty little head of yours." He arched a brow. "Because I care about you too, but you're going to see me get all weird about it."

She narrowed her stare. "I'm not being strange."

"Oh. Yes, you are."

She blew out a puff of air directly upward. Some of her hair shifted.

Toby took her into his arms, pulling her back against his chest. His lips pressed against her neck.

"I can't think straight when you do that."

"What has you spooked?" He sucked on her earlobe.

"That's not a good way to get me talking." She groaned, dropping her head back to his shoulder. "Where do you see us in a year?"

"Is that what this is all about? The future and if we have one?"

"Kind of."

He rested his chin on her shoulder. "You're unexpected and you came into my life when everything else turned upside down."

"I don't think I'm going to like the way—"

"Don't jump to conclusions. It's not a good look on you." He covered her mouth with his hand. "You stepped right in to help me with TJ. Before anything happened between us—you've been there for me and my son. It took me a while to separate what went from you being a babysitter, to my friend, to someone I had deep feelings for."

Zinny closed her eyes and listened to the timbre of his voice and the words that tumbled from his lips. She focused on the meaning, and not where her mind and imagination tried to take her, because that was a dangerous headspace. She could talk herself right out of the tub and out the door. Maybe things would end and perhaps that was best.

But she owed it to him to hear every single syllable and how he meant them because she'd put herself in this position.

"However, I have that all straight in my head and while I don't have a crystal ball and I can't tell you what things will look like for us in six months or a year, I can tell you I want you to be in my life and not as a friend."

She inhaled sharply. Her chest tightened. "I hate to bring this up, but what if Serena doesn't go to jail? What if she gets off scot-free?"

"As in found innocent of all charges?"

"Yes."

"That's not going to affect you and me," Toby said, running his hands up and down her arms. His lips went back to kissing her neck. "I'm still getting divorced."

"But it might affect the custody arrangement of TJ."

"It could." His hands came up under the swell of her breasts. "But that doesn't change our relationship."

"I wouldn't ever want to be the person who got between you and your son."

"I know that." He turned her to face him and took her chin in his thumb and forefinger. "I want you to stop worrying about this stuff and let's enjoy this night. When TJ moves into the dorms, there will be more nights. We have a future. I don't know exactly what it looks like, but know that I'm falling head over heels for you, Zinfandel River, and I have no intention of letting you and all this gorgeous red hair walk out of my life anytime soon." He took her mouth in a hot, fiery kiss. His fingers dug into her flesh, tugging her tight to his body. He lifted her right out of the tub and wrapped a towel around her body before carrying her off into the bedroom.

He set her on the mattress, pulling back the covers. He kissed her sensitive skin from head to toe. He took his sweet time, not letting any inch go unnoticed. His touch was exquisite. Every time they made love it was different. Sometimes it was hard and fast. Other times it was fun and flirty.

But it was always sex.

Tonight it was more than that. Her head spun with all the emotion that spilled from his body to hers.

He seemed to take more interest in her pleasure than his own.

"Toby," she whispered as she curled her fingers around him.

He tried to bat her hand away, but she wasn't going to allow that to happen. Not this time. She wanted to hear her name roll off his soft lips while she drove him crazy.

"Please. Let me."

"I'm not going to stop you," he managed between ragged breaths. "Only, you can't do this for very long or this will be the end of it."

She glanced up and smiled. "I've never felt so powerful."

He growled. "You've always had control over me." He lay on his back, propped up on his pillow with his hand behind his head and the other holding her hair out of the way.

This hadn't necessarily been her favorite thing to do while making love. It wasn't that she opposed to the physical act. She wasn't. However, she had a boyfriend once who had pushed her head so hard she gagged and choked.

She didn't like that.

If she was going to do this, it would always be on her own terms and she loved that Toby relaxed into it and let her have at him in the way that made her happy, but pleased him as well.

He guided her, but he didn't force her in any way.

His muscles flexed and he whispered her name.

It was like hearing the angels sing.

"I'm sorry, Zinny. But I need you to stop."

She wiped her lips and smiled. "That was fun."

"I'm not going to disagree. But we're far from over." He reached for the condoms and wrapped himself. "Come here."

She climbed on top of him, easing him inside slowly, arching her back, enjoying every electric pulse that he created.

He leaned closer, drawing her nipple into his mouth, swirling his tongue over the hard nub. His hips moved with hers in perfect unison. Each knew exactly what the other needed and when to bring them just to the brink of ecstasy.

Her orgasm hit first.

His followed seconds later.

Their bodies rocked together in perfect harmony.

She shuddered as she collapsed to his chest.

His arms came around her body, his fingers running up and down her spine, making her tingle.

She closed her eyes tight, trying not to let her mind wander again, but it was impossible. She'd fallen in love with Toby. That was a fact. His kid too. She wanted to spend the rest of her life with both of them.

And she understood what that meant.

People could say she was too young all they wanted. That she hadn't lived enough to understand, but she did. Having been raised by the Weezer made sure of that. Her life experiences were unique and she hadn't been living under a rock. No one coddled her growing up. Nope. She might as well have been tossed to the wolves. Even though she was the baby and daddy's little girl, she still had to learn many of life's lessons the hard way.

She sighed. "Can I ask you something?"

"Of course." Shifting her to the side, he pulled the covers over her body.

"It's serious."

"Does this require strawberries and champagne? Because we left those in the bathroom," he asked.

"That might be a good idea."

"I'll be right back."

She pulled the sheet to her chin. Earlier, she'd allowed the conversation to be cut short because Toby had believed he'd covered what she needed.

And for the most part, he had.

There was no reason for her to be jealous.

He cared about her and believed this relationship had legs.

But what did that look like long term? She needed to know only one thing and that wasn't if he loved her.

He might not be ready to express that, if he even did. However, she believed they were headed down that road, yet it wouldn't do her any good if he couldn't see a similar future.

He returned with the bottle, both glasses, and the bowl of fruit.

She took one of the glasses and chugged.

"You were thirsty."

"I sure was." She laughed, waiting for him to pour more.

"So, what's your question?" He climbed back in bed. "You better ask away before I get a second wind."

"Oh my. Aren't you feeling frisky and like a seventeen-year-old boy."

"Frisky, yes, but not seventeen; that's for damn sure."

She laughed.

"I'm waiting." He arched a brow.

"I'm just curious, but would you ever consider having more kids?"

He coughed, pounding on his chest.

"I take it that's a no." She downed another full glass of her adult beverage.

"You'd take it wrong." He took the glass from her hand and set it on the nightstand. "You just caught me off guard," he said. "I wanted to have more kids, but Serena lied to me about birth control, and then I didn't want to have more with her. When I filed for divorce, I just figured that ship had sailed. But I take it that having children is something you want?"

"I do," she admitted. She'd brought this up, so there was no point in lying. "It would be nice to have one or two."

He ran a hand across the top of his head. "I guess this is where our age difference shows."

"You wouldn't have more?"

"I didn't say that. But I'm also about to send TJ to high school. I'm forty. I'm not getting any younger and I wouldn't want to wait much longer if I were to do and —well—we're just not ready for this conversation."

"I'm sorry. I can't help it. But when I think of my future, I think about three things. Working at the family winery with my siblings. Getting married. And having a kid or two."

He reached out and palmed her cheek. "As you should, if that's what you want. However, until I know for certain where things are with Serena and whether or not she's going to jail, and then where custody stands, I can't think past the next few months. I know that's not fair to you."

"Toby. It's okay. I shouldn't have even brought all this up. You've got more important things to deal with. But we've never been alone this long." Did she just say that out loud? Holy shit. That was a huge statement.

His eyes grew wide. "Yes, we have. And you are important to me too. Don't ever forget that. Just because—"

"I know my place in your life."

"Don't toss my words back at me," Toby said. "Yes. TJ comes first. I appreciate you understanding and accepting that. But that doesn't mean you—"

She covered his mouth. "We need to drop this subject because we're going in circles. All we can do is get through tomorrow and take things one day at a time." The real reason she wanted to stop talking about it was because the longer they did, the more chance she had at crying. Toby was being as sweet as a peach pie. But the reality was he danced around the subject. He didn't commit because he couldn't and not because he was still married or that custody was still in question when it came to TJ.

It was because Toby didn't know if he could have another child.

This Zinny believed with all of her heart.

He pulled his lips together in a tight line. "All right," he said, wrapping his arms around her and tugging her to his chest. "Shall we watch a show while I regain some stamina?"

"Sounds like a plan." Falling in love, as wonderful as that feeling was, had its pitfalls when her vision for the future didn't mesh with his.

8

TOBY

Toby stood in the courthouse hallway and glanced at his watch. The proceedings had been pushed back over an hour and he hadn't heard from or seen Levi for the last thirty minutes. Toby understood that things ran late and that the judge had other cases she was presiding over today.

Only, all this waiting around gave Toby's mind a chance to wander back to last night and Zinny's questions about the future.

Specifically, her declaration that she wanted a baby.

A baby.

He should have thought of that before he allowed anything to happen with Zinny. He'd been concerned about hurting her because she was so young and he didn't know what his future looked like.

He still didn't.

However, he'd gotten over that hurdle. He saw her as an adult, capable of making her own grown-up decisions, including climbing into bed with anyone she chose.

And she chose him.

He wasn't using her for sex. He truly cared for her in ways he hadn't expected. If he dared to be honest— he was falling in love with Zinny and that scared the fuck out of him.

Could he do another kid in his forties? He'd wanted another child in the worst way after he and Serena had TJ. For ten years he thought they tried but that had all been a farce. Serena had lied. When he confronted her about it, she came up with a million reasons why she hadn't wanted another baby, but not a good reason to lie about it.

He'd been devastated.

Their marriage had never been the same. Of course, she'd been cheating on him so there was that too.

A door opened down the hall.

He jerked his head.

But it wasn't Levi or anyone to do with Serena's case.

"Relax," Carter said, who had come for moral support. This was the State of New Jersey versus Serena Tillman.

Toby would be called to testify, eventually, but other than that, he had nothing to do with it. The outcome would affect custody and he was torn by that. He wanted TJ to live with him and he wanted to be the only one making decisions about TJ's future.

But he didn't want TJ's mother to go to prison for the simple fact that TJ was going to have to live with that burden.

However, Serena deserved that punishment for what she did to Chablis.

"Easier said than done." Toby stuffed his hands in his pockets and let out a long breath. "Until this is over, I will be on edge. You don't know Serena like I do." He raked a hand across the top of his head. "I'm going to take that back. I'm learning I didn't know her at all."

"I hate to be the one to tell this to you, son. But you're just starting to see her true colors."

Toby had been fourteen when he first started dating Serena. That was twenty-six years ago. What he saw then was a girl who came to his hockey games, cheered him on, and let him touch her boobs behind the bleachers. He was a kid who acted like one.

But he knew then she had a mean streak. He saw it, and he ignored it. Not because he liked her, though it took him years to figure this out, but because it was what his father expected him to do. His dad wanted Toby to be the best and the only way to do that was to beat Dax.

However, Toby wasn't quite as good as Dax was on the ice and Toby had an attitude problem.

"Trust me, I know what she's capable of. I only wish

I hadn't been turning a blind eye for so long all in the name of trying to protect my son."

Carter reached out and squeezed Toby's biceps. "Don't beat yourself up over that. You're a good father. You've done right by that kid and it shows."

"Thank you for that, but I'm not so sure sometimes." Toby folded his arms across his chest. "Once we made the decision to allow TJ to play travel hockey, I saw the old Serena come out. It was so important for her to see TJ be the best. I just wanted him to have fun. At first, she seemed like she could get on board with that. But she got caught up in the politics and I found myself right behind her. When I saw how much real talent TJ had, I started pushing. I was reliving my childhood through him and wanted so badly for TJ to have his shot."

"There's nothing wrong with that."

"Maybe not, but there's a lot wrong with the way I went about it and how I ignored certain things."

"That may be true, but you're doing things differently now and if you think Serena might not have gone down this road, think again."

Toby rubbed the back of his neck. He couldn't take any responsibility for her actions. Deep down, he knew that, but part of him wondered if he'd made better choices if she would have too.

"This wasn't just about getting TJ on the CWF Prep hockey team for Brooks," Carter continued. "This was about ruining Dax. Destroying his career because of what he did to Brooks. I'm sorry if I'm being harsh, but that's a reality you need to keep in the forefront of your mind as we move forward."

"You're right." Toby nodded. Serena didn't care about anyone but herself and at the time all this went down, she thought Brooks was going to steal the job away from Dax and step in and be a father to TJ and a husband to her.

Only, Brooks never had any intention of stepping up to the plate. All he wanted was to hurt Dax any way he could. That started with taking Dax's position as head coach and destroying Chablis' reputation. Brooks made it very clear that day at the rink that he had no desire to be a father. Serena had been a means to an end.

Period.

"I've been doing this a long time," Carter said. "Levi has a strong case and he's told me in confidence that Serena's lawyer has tried to get her to take that plea deal, but that it's Serena digging her heels in."

"I don't want her to go to jail." Toby's mind flashed to the day TJ was born. It had been a difficult labor. Eighteen hours of Serena screaming and yelling at everyone who came near her. All she wanted was to get that baby out of her body. She begged for drugs. And when she got them, she still complained even though she was no longer in enormous pain. She couldn't understand why they wouldn't just take her to the operating room and *cut that kid right out* as she put it. Toby had made the mistake of laughing. He'd tried to mask it by covering his mouth and turning, but Serena had heard it and she laid into him like there was no tomorrow.

She nearly kicked him out.

Childbirth had not been what Serena had expected. It took a lot out of her and for a few weeks after, she didn't want to even hold TJ. The doctors told Toby that was normal, but to make sure Serena spoke with a professional, which he did. Things got better, but as Toby had been forced to examine every detail of his marriage, he realized that Serena tended to use their son as a pawn and a weapon.

It wasn't that he didn't think she loved him because he knew without a doubt she did. She wasn't a soulless person. She was capable of caring about others. But her happiness came first and that was a cold fact that Toby had finally accepted.

"That only punishes my son more," Toby said. "Correct me if I'm wrong, but the plea deal still gets her a felony charge and will help me in my custody case."

"Absolutely." Carter lifted his finger. "However, a conviction with jail time would ensure full custody. With the plea deal, we run the risk of joint custody being granted."

"But with a trial she could be found not guilty."

Carter nodded. "I get how hard this is for you. That's the mother of your precious son and that changes everything. Not to mention her crime wasn't violent."

Toby shook his head. "What she did is inexcusable and she should be held accountable. I don't like that TJ is learning a life lesson at the expense of his mom's actions, but that's the reality."

"That's the only way to look at this."

Toby leaned against the wall and stared at the ceiling. He forced himself to think of something more positive.

Zinny.

But that circled his thoughts back to having another baby. "Carter. Can I ask you a non-legal question?"

"Sure."

"How old were you when you had Malbec?"

Carter narrowed his stare. "Twenty-three. Why?"

"So, that means you were forty-one when you had Zinny?"

Carter took three steps in Toby's direction. "Are you trying to tell me something, son?"

"No. Oh, my God. No." Toby held up his hands. He glanced left and right. "Zinny's not... she's not... you know."

"Good. But are you asking me this because she wants to have children and you don't?" His tone was darker than it had been at his house yesterday.

And this time it was serious.

"I didn't say that. I mean, yeah. She wants kids. However, between everything with us being so new and not knowing what TJ's future is going to be when it comes to custody and all this looming over my head, I hadn't thought about that part when I got involved, and now I'm feeling like a jerk."

"Oh. I see." Carter smirked.

Actually smirked as if he enjoyed this moment.

Toby had to admit, if he had a daughter, he probably would too.

"You should feel like an ass." Carter turned and took a seat on the bench, folding his arms. "But since we're on the subject, are you concerned you're too old?"

"A little."

"Isn't Malbec your age?"

"He is," Toby said.

"He's having a baby and I know he and Eliza Jane want to have another one. Dax and Chablis are trying. Riesling is only a few years younger, and I believe Trey is closer to your age. Not to mention that if it had been up to me, we would have had at least one more after Zinny. I wanted an even number of kids, but Weezer had a really bad pregnancy with that one and the delivery wasn't that great either. The doctor told us no more." Carter shrugged. "So, that was the end of the baby-making train for us." Carter sighed. "Not that I'm giving you permission or anything. Just so you have it clear in your head, my shotgun is in my truck."

"Oh. That's crystal clear."

"Good," Carter said.

The door to the judge's chambers swung open and Levi stepped out into the hallway followed by Serena and her lawyer.

Serena had the audacity to smile and wave.

Toby ignored her altogether.

Carter jumped to his feet.

Levi tucked a file under his arm and took long strides in their direction. He was a tall man. About six two or six three. He had short blond hair with almond eyes.

Toby could see why Zinny had been attracted to him, at least in the looks department. Even though he was arrogant as hell, Toby found him to be a decent sort of fellow, except when it came to what Zinny had told him about his family.

That, Toby couldn't understand.

He could never walk away from his son or allow Serena to take his kid away from him. Toby's chest tightened. Serena wasn't going to give in without a fight. The question was, what would be her angle? And how low would she go?

"Well, I've got good news and bad news," Levi said. "What do you want first?"

"The good." Carter didn't give Toby a chance to answer.

Toby swallowed. His pulse pounded between his ears. He had no idea what was happening.

"Serena and her lawyer begged me to put the plea offer back on the table." Levi lifted his brow. "I told them I'd do it, but it meant it wasn't as good of an offer anymore. I tacked on another three months and a public apology."

"Did she take it?" Toby asked.

Levi nodded. "She didn't even bat an eyelash. Signed right on the dotted line."

"That is good news," Carter said. "So, what's the bad?"

"I don't know to deliver this lightly, so I'm just going to say it." Levi glanced over his shoulder. "She's filing paperwork right now to sue you for full custody."

"Fuck," Carter muttered. "I better go file ours now."

"Wait. That's only the beginning." Levi held up the folder in his hands. "She wants me to open two criminal cases, which I'm going to have to at least investigate and so is social services."

"I don't like the sound of this," Carter said.

Toby's stomach churned.

"The first one is that Toby has abused TJ." Levi flipped through some pages. "She gave me three different incidents. A broken wrist. A black eye. And stitches on his calf."

"I never touched my son." Toby clenched his fists. "I can tell you exactly what happened on each of those injuries and it wasn't because I hurt him."

"I'm not saying you did." Levi held his stare. "I'm telling you what she's alleging and the fact it has to be looked into, which brings me to the second thing she's accusing you of."

Carter put his hand on Toby's shoulder as if that would hold his emotions down.

"This should be good," Toby whispered.

"I can't believe I have to say this out loud, especially in present company." Levi sucked in a deep breath and let it out slowly. "But Serena suggested that you had an affair with Zinny when she was underage."

"Are you fucking kidding me?" Toby's blood turned to fire.

"I wish I were," Levi said. "She's stating that you've been having an affair with Zinny on and off for a few years." Levi closed his eyes for a moment. "I'll have to chime in and state for the record that I was dating Zinny during the time frame that she believes that was going on, but that only helps your divorce and not custody."

"She's the devil," Carter said. "I knew she'd play dirty, but this goes way below the belt."

"Mr. River, it gets worse. She says she has proof that Toby took advantage of Zinny when she was a teenager."

"That's impossible. I'm going to fucking—"

"Don't finish that statement, Toby," Levi said. "She played us and she did a good job of that. Even the judge was annoyed, but happy this wasn't going to trial. She was thrilled Serena came to her senses, but not so excited to hear the rest of this bullshit. She found it calculated. She even said so, but she had to call social services."

"What's going to happen now? Can they take TJ from me?" Toby's heart fell to his feet like a cement brick taking him to the bottom of the ocean. His throat closed up.

"If you're asking if they will remove him based on an accusation, the answer is no," Carter said. "They will, however, come to the house, speak to you, and speak to TJ. They will interview others as well, including the doctors who treated TJ. It will be painful, but the truth is on our side."

"What about the bullshit she's saying about me and Zinny?" Toby made sure he looked Carter in the eye. "I swear to you, I never—"

"I know that, son," Carter said. "Serena had to have found out about you and Zinny somehow and now she's trying to use it against you in a custody battle that's going to get about as ugly as one can get."

"So, you and Zinny are a thing?" Levi asked.

Toby nodded. But maybe they shouldn't be. Perhaps he should put the whole thing on pause.

"Both of these allegations are things I'm duty bound to have the proper authorities explore. There is no statute of limitations on rape in New Jersey." Levi tucked the folder back under his arm. "I resent I'm having to use resources on a bullshit case when I know perfectly well you didn't do anything you're being accused of, but I can't ignore it either."

"Is this really happening?" Toby stared at Carter.

"Unfortunately, it is," Carter said, turning his attention to Levi. "Thank you for giving us the heads-up."

"I will keep you in the loop." Levi stretched out his hand. "I'll make sure TJ is assigned a lawyer I know personally."

"TJ will need a lawyer?" The air in Toby's lungs flew out like wind crashing into the shore.

"In all custody cases that go to court, the minor is represented by their own attorney to make sure their interests are truly met," Levi said. "I'll be in touch."

"This is crazy," Toby mumbled.

"I won't disagree," Carter said.

"I can't believe I'm going to ask this, but do I need to call things off with Zinny? As much as I don't want to hurt my son, I don't want to put her in the line of fire either."

"It's a little late for that and my daughter is a grown woman. She can make her own decisions and if she wants to be with you, then I stand by her, so my short answer is no. There is no reason for you and Zinny to break up. But there is also no reason for you to flaunt it around town either." Carter squeezed his shoulder. "I've dealt with people like Serena before. I need you to trust me and let me do the job you've hired me to do, okay?"

"It's not that," Toby said. "It's the fact that TJ is going to be exposed to all these lies. His mother is going to put him through hell, and for what? To get back at me?" Toby had felt pure anger before, but never in his life had rage filled his heart. "She doesn't care about TJ or what's best for him. If she did, she wouldn't be doing this."

"You're right," Carter said. "Unfortunately, that makes her very dangerous. Not only does she have nothing to lose, but she doesn't care who she hurts on the way to get what she wants. The problem I'm having is I don't believe her only motivation is to hurt you. There has to be more to this that we're missing. Regardless, I need you to be willing to fight as dirty as she is."

"I won't do anything that could hurt TJ," Toby said. "My job is to protect him."

"In order for you to do that, you need to keep him from Serena. Therefore, I need you to dig deep and find me all the things that make her a bad mother."

Toby lowered his chin to his chest. "That's going to hurt TJ. While he struggles with his mom right now, he still loves her. How can I do that to him?"

"Because if you don't, you might lose him to her."

Zinny

Zinny sat on one side of the picnic bench on the back patio of the winery while TJ sat at on the other side and stared at his phone. He'd been looking at it since she picked him up from school and he wouldn't stop.

When she asked, he admitted he was looking for information about the case.

Toby told her not to take the cell away. He would find out what happened regardless. At least he would be in good company.

"Are you sure you don't want to go with Malbec and Merlot into the vineyards? They are preparing for the harvest and that's pretty cool." Ever since she'd picked up the boy from school, he'd been quiet. He'd answered all her questions about the sleepover and he didn't seem to hold any information back, but he wasn't himself.

She understood, considering today his mother was pleading not guilty to felony charges and a judge would be setting a date for her to face a jury of her peers. Scratch that. She had no idea what that was like. Her mother was a lot of things and growing up, Zinny had to learn at a very young age to let things roll off her back. Being the Weezer's daughter wasn't easy. It wasn't hard, but it did take a strong back.

Her mom hadn't ever done anything that got her arrested though.

"No. I'm good." TJ kept his head down and he continued to scroll on the screen. "Didn't you say my dad would be here soon?"

She glanced at her watch, wondering what the hell was taking Toby so long. Today was just supposed to be about setting a date for trial. Both he and her dad told her that it should be a quick appearance and they should be out by three.

It was nearly five and she hadn't heard from either of them. Nor had there been anything on the news, and she'd signed up for alerts.

Her heart dropped to the pit of her stomach. As much as she wanted Serena to pay for what she'd done to Chablis, Zinny felt horrible for TJ. Serena's crime didn't change the fact that she was still TJ's mother and her possibly going to prison for any length of time would impact his life negatively. There was no denying that.

Then there was the divorce.

Her parents had been divorced for years when she'd been born. As a matter of fact, she never knew what life was like when they'd been married. Or lived together. So, she had no idea what TJ was feeling. She wished she could relate to his emotions. To help guide him through this phase in his life, but she felt helpless.

And if she felt that way, she could only imagine what Toby had to be going through when it came to his son.

It had been hard to gauge.

Eliza Jane waddled out the tasting room door, rubbing her round belly. She was due in a couple of weeks, but if you asked her, she looked and felt like she was due last month.

She carried a couple of sodas and a box of cheese crackers. "I thought TJ might like a snack."

"Thanks." Zinny tapped TJ on the shoulder.

He grunted, barely acknowledging the nice gesture. TJ could be a moody kid, but not usually around the River family. He genuinely seemed to enjoy their company. He engaged in activities and conversation.

But not today.

She wanted to press him to have good manners, but decided to let it slide. He knew what was happening and he hadn't seen his mom since that day at the ice rink. He had to be scared and confused.

And obviously angry.

Though the poor kid had internalized that pain and currently wasn't taking it out on anyone. Toby had found a therapist for TJ, but it wasn't any of her business to ask how it had gone.

Zinny walked with Eliza Jane back to the main building.

"Poor kid," Eliza Jane said while she rubbed her stomach. "I can't imagine what he must be thinking."

"This is just the beginning." Zinny glanced over her shoulder. "My dad said a trial in this case would only be about a day or two."

"I heard she faces up to five years."

"My dad doesn't believe she'll get that long. Eighteen months tops, but that's all putting the cart before the horse. My dad was just giving Toby his opinions and making it clear that he really didn't know what might happen." Zinny let out a long sigh. "TJ is so quiet today and it concerns me. We talked about this before we dropped him off for the overnight. He knows this is just a hearing to set the date. A formality. He knows nothing is happening and yet, he's looking at the phone and scrolling for news as if something is."

"Maybe he's worried the media will turn this into a nightmare for his dad." Eliza Jane leaned forward and made a strange noise.

"Are you okay?"

"Yeah. I get these false labor pains. They suck, but the doctor assures me that I'll know the difference. However, I told Malbec, if real labor is worse than this, he's going to hear his wife call him the most horrible names in the world. Worse than the Weezer could ever come up with."

"Oh. I want to be in the labor and delivery room for that."

"Not going to happen." Eliza Jane tilted her head and glared. "Malbec is lucky he gets to join this party."

Zinny laughed, but it was cut short when her phone buzzed in her pocket. She pulled it out and glanced at the screen. "It's Toby." She swallowed her pulse. "Hey," she said. "How did things go in court?"

"Is TJ in earshot?"

"No," she said.

"Serena took the plea deal after all."

"I understood Levi would offer again, but I thought that would be a formality." Zinny didn't often find her father's job interesting. Normally she found it boring as hell. Dry, to be exact. But someone had to be a lawyer and her dad was damn good at it.

"That's what I thought, but as I've learned, this isn't me against Serena; it's the State of New Jersey," Toby said with a fair amount of disgust. "She lost her nursing license and she can never work in the medical field. Not even as a receptionist in a doctor's office."

"Wait. What? Are you telling me she's not getting any time at all?" Zinny whispered, covering her mouth over the cell.

Eliza Jane squeezed her biceps.

"Three years probation, which is a little longer than the original plea deal, one year mandatory therapy, and she has to make a very public apology to Chablis, Dax, and the medical community."

"Thank God for small favors," Zinny mumbled. The entire thing was a catch-22. Her family was vindicated. But TJ paid the price for his mother's mistake. It didn't matter that it wasn't his fault; it would be a dark shadow that followed him because people were assholes.

"That's the only good news in this scenario," Toby said.

"Zinny." Her mother stuck her head out the door. "Get in here."

"I'm on the phone," she said.

"I don't care." Weezer took her by the arm and tugged.

"What the hell is going on?" She blinked.

"My mom's giving a press conference." TJ came barreling into the wine making room. The television in the corner was turned on to a *breaking news* special.

Serena stood behind a podium. To her right was her lawyer and to her left was fucking Brooks Halsteder.

"Toby. Where are you?" Zinny inched closer to TJ and put her arm around his shoulders.

He leaned close, as if he needed her support.

"I'm just getting in my car, why?"

"Serena's giving—"

"Holy shit. I see her," Toby muttered.

"Turn it up, Ma," Zinny said.

"I pleaded guilty to violating HIPAA laws today," Serena said. *Halsteder stood by her side. He didn't smile. He didn't touch her. He just stood there looking like the asshole that he was.*

What the fuck was he doing back in town?

"I do want to apologize to Chablis River for what I did. I know it was wrong. However, it should be known that my motivation was to protect my son from a predator."

"What is she doing?" Zinny's mother asked.

Zinny wished she knew. She pressed the cell to her ear, but Toby said nothing. She squeezed TJ's shoulder. He was as stiff as a board.

"I have remained silent until now because I have felt powerless. It is difficult to be in an abusive relationship."

Zinny gasped. "She did not just say that."

"I cannot get into all the details because the district attor-

ney's office is opening an investigation, but my soon-to-be ex-husband is the real criminal here. He's violent and should be in jail. I'm going to make sure that happens and so will TJ's real father, Brooks Halsteder."

"Brooks is my biological father?" TJ took a step back and glared at Zinny.

"Give TJ the phone," Toby yelled.

Zinny held it out to TJ. "It's your dad," she said softly. Tears burned her eyes. She couldn't imagine what was going through TJ's head, or his heart, right now.

"Brooks or Toby?" TJ asked with a hardness to his tone.

"It's your father," Zinny said behind a tight jaw. She wasn't going to play that game. She knew the boy was hurting, but Toby was the man who had raised him. The one who took responsibility when Brooks didn't. The one who would always be there for him, and Brooks would never be that man.

He ran out on TJ fourteen years ago.

And he did so again just a month ago.

What made anyone think Brooks would stick around for any length of time? Serena promised him something; otherwise, why would he even stick his neck out? It made no sense.

"I don't want to talk to any of them. They are all a bunch of liars." TJ smacked her hand. The cell went flying across the room. He turned on his heel and ran out the door.

"I'll go after him." Weezer didn't give Zinny a chance to argue.

Zinny picked up the cell. "Toby?"

"I'm here. What happened?"

"He ran out of the building. My mom's chasing after him." She pulled up one of the stools and sat down. "He can't get too far."

Eliza Jane came up next to her and took her hand. "It's going to be okay," she whispered.

"I think Serena texted him she was going to give a statement." Zinny sighed. "I can't believe she did that."

"I'll be there in less than fifteen minutes. Your dad is right behind me. Do you know if TJ has his cell still?"

"Let me check." Zinny raced outside. TJ's backpack was on the picnic table. So was his phone. "No. He doesn't."

"Thanks. I'll be there soon."

Zinny leaned forward, pressing her hands on the wood top. Tears flowed freely from her eyes to her cheeks. Her heart broke into a million pieces for TJ. He knew that Toby had adopted him when he'd been born. He understood that his biological father hadn't wanted to be in his life. Toby had told Zinny that TJ hadn't asked too many questions over the years about who his biological father had been, but that every once in a while, the topic would come up.

He and Serena had agreed that if he asked when he was an adult, they would tell him the truth.

That reality was only four years away.

But to find out by his mother giving a press conference on television?

That was brutal.

And mean.

She wiped her tears and squared her shoulders. She needed to be strong for TJ and Toby. They needed her and she wouldn't let them down.

Ever.

9

———

TOBY

Toby had half a mind to turn his vehicle around have it out with both Serena and Brooks, but that wouldn't do him any good except maybe give credence to the story line that Serena was trying to build that he was a violent man.

Which wasn't true.

Even on the ice Dax had been more of a physical player than Toby had been, though Toby had dropped the gloves a few times.

What hockey player hadn't?

He pulled into the winery and parked next to Zinny's car. He couldn't imagine what kind of so-called evidence Serena had of him having an inappropriate relationship with Zinny when she'd been a kid, but he couldn't focus on that right now. His immediate problem was the fact that Brooks had been outed as TJ's biological father and what that meant.

Worse, the idea that Brooks and Serena were now a united front.

Or the fact that if he wanted to be one with Zinny, it was tainted by this crazy-ass idea that he would have ever gotten involved with her when she'd been a child.

He shivered at the thought.

Only, the number of years she'd been an adult kept jumping in his mind. He had to remind himself he hadn't done anything wrong. If he had, the Weezer and Carter would have surely shot him by now.

Yes. There was an age difference.

So what.

His dad had been ten years older than his mom.

The current chief of police was twelve years older than his wife.

It wasn't a horrible thing and he wasn't going to let Serena make him feel like it was. Or use it to turn his son against him, though this Brooks thing might actually do that well enough.

Fuck. His mind had been jumbled for the last twenty minutes and he couldn't think straight. He'd broken up with Zinny a dozen times in his head and each time his heart broke. Or he heard Carter's voice telling him not to let Serena drive the narrative. Carter had told him twice since he left the courthouse that Serena was going to say and do things that made him— or Zinny—look bad and Toby was going to have to bite his tongue.

That was going to be no easy task.

He had no idea how Carter remained calm because all Toby wanted to do was hit Serena where it counted. If she wanted to fight dirty, he could too.

But Carter told him he had to be the bigger person and keep his mouth closed.

He entered the gift shop, which thankfully didn't have too many people, though the few that were in there turned and stared before whispering amongst themselves.

Fucking wonderful. It had already started.

"Hey, Toby," Malbec greeted him with an outstretched hand. "My sister's out back on the picnic benches waiting for you."

"Do we know where my son is?" While Toby needed to talk with Zinny, he needed to know TJ was okay.

"He's up by the alpaca farm. My mom is with him."

"How do I get there?"

Malbec pointed to doors on the other side of the counter. "Go through there. Zinny can show you how to get to where the alpacas hang out near the property line."

"Thanks." Toby strolled toward the back entrance.

"Toby?" Malbec called.

"Yeah?" Toby glanced over his shoulder.

"We are all here for you and TJ. Every single one of us. Whatever you need, all you have to do is ask."

"I appreciate that." Toby sucked in a deep breath as he stepped through the doors.

Zinny sat on the picnic table, her hair pulled back

into a ponytail. She wore little to no makeup, which was normal for her and one of the things he loved about her.

Loved.

She had become important to him in such a short time.

No. That wasn't entirely true. He had been relying on her for the last year and fighting his feelings for at least that long.

"I'm so sorry." She jumped to her feet, but didn't come any closer. It was as if she could read his trepidation.

"It's not your fault." He reached out and pulled her in for a brief hug. He wanted to hold her for longer, but he feared people were watching. He shouldn't care.

But he did. Not for his sake, but for hers.

And TJ's.

They were who mattered.

"Where's TJ's phone?" he asked.

"Right there." She nodded toward TJ's backpack.

Toby hated the distance he'd put between him and Zinny. It tore his heart in half. He'd fallen in love with her and he needed her support. He sat on the edge of the table and tapped the passcode.

"Does TJ know that you can access his cell?" Zinny asked.

"Yes," he admitted. "It was the deal we made with him when we got him a smartphone. If he changed it, no more cell."

"That's smart." Zinny adjusted her ponytail. "Had I known what Serena was going to do, I wouldn't have let him—"

"You couldn't have known, and he would have found out anyway." Toby glanced up, catching her gaze. "I'm glad he was here with all of you. I know he raced out, but he's in a safe space, and I'm grateful for that."

"I didn't go after him. I should have."

Toby shook his head. "You're too close." He scrolled through the text messages from Serena to his kid and that rage that had filled his veins now circled into his heart. "He wouldn't have listened to you, though I can't imagine what he and the Weezer might be talking about."

"Yeah. That's a scary thought, but why don't you think he wouldn't open up to me?"

"Because Serena is trying to poison him against you." He swallowed the bile that bubbled from the back of his throat.

Your adopted father doesn't care about you. He's going to dump you at CWF Prep so he can be with his girlfriend.

Zinny doesn't care about you. She's after my family's money. Don't let her fool you. She seduced your dad and she wants to get rid of you. Next thing you know, she'll be sending you off to summer programs. I bet they signed you up for Dax's summer hockey program.

He didn't want to hurt Zinny, but she was going to find all this out eventually. She might as well hear it now. He handed her the cell. "I have a lot of explaining to do with TJ about his biological father first, but I will set him straight about you as well."

Zinny took the phone. Her eyes went wide. "She's taking truths and twisting them."

"I know," Toby said. "Serena has always been good at that." Toby took Zinny's hand and kissed her palm. "Have you talked with your dad?"

"I have." She took her free hand and wiped the tears that dribbled down her cheeks.

In all the years he'd known Zinny, he didn't think he'd ever seen her cry. She'd always been a ray of sunshine. Full of positive energy.

He wrapped his arm around her and pulled her close. Carter had told him there was no reason he and Zinny couldn't be together. Of course, that was before the press conference. Before TJ found out about Brooks.

But that didn't change how Toby felt about Zinny.

It only changed how Carter moved forward with his side of the custody hearing.

And how he dealt with TJ, because honestly, if TJ responded badly, he would have to back off. That might not be fair to Zinny—or to him—but TJ was the priority.

"I feel like I've entered some weird alternate universe," Zinny said. "My father didn't give me all the details, but enough. Serena better cross the road when she sees me coming."

"Zinny, don't give her any ammunition. Promise me?"

"You sound like my father."

"And don't remind me of our age difference," he said with a long breath. "I walked back here with every intention of telling you that we can't see each other."

"My dad told me you might do that and he thinks that's a mistake."

Toby rubbed his temples.

Zinny ran her hand up and down his spine. "I don't know what the right thing to do is. If we stop being together, we're giving in to Serena. It's like she wins. She's in control. But I don't want to do anything that will hurt TJ and ever since I picked him up at school, he was staring at the phone. I had no idea he was looking at texts from his mother."

"If I were in your shoes, I'd run. And fast. Serena is going to drag you through the mud." Toby shifted, facing Zinny. His brain had been in hyperdrive ever since he'd left the courthouse. He'd waffled back and forth on his relationship with Zinny, and the bottom line was he agreed with Carter.

Serena had nothing because there was nothing. Even the allegations of child abuse were all smoke and mirrors.

She wanted this to play out in the court of public opinion.

Serena's goal with Chablis' abortion records had been to humiliate Chablis and make everyone judge her for making that choice when she'd been a young adult.

Worse, making that decision without telling the father.

She thought Dax would become so enraged he'd quit his job and leave Candlewood Falls. Or the school would fire him because of what Chablis had done.

But all that backfired on Serena.

While there were a few in town who judged Chablis for her choice, it hadn't quite had the effect Serena had hoped for and the tabloids shifted to her story and what she'd done.

Serena didn't like that, not to mention she faced jail time.

"I'm not afraid of Serena," Zinny said with a fair amount of conviction.

One of the many reasons Toby had fallen in love with her.

"She's going to uncover every dark secret you have and use it against me." Toby wasn't trying to scare Zinny away. He simply wanted her to be totally aware of what was in store. "She's going to use you to make me look like an unfit father."

"Are you asking me if there is anything in my past that can hurt you?"

He jerked his head back. "Well, no. That wasn't where I was going with this."

"But now that I mention it?" She arched a brow. "I've smoked pot," she said. "I drank before I was twenty-one. But my family owns a winery, so there's that."

Toby laughed. "I'm not asking for a list."

"Yeah, well, I'm sure she can find something and make it look nasty as hell."

"Agreed," he said. "I need to go find TJ and figure out where his head is at and what our next move is. I'll text you later, okay?"

She palmed his cheek. "Please tell TJ I'm always here for him if he wants to talk."

"I will do that." He leaned in and brushed his lips over her mouth. He wished he could let them linger longer. "This is going to be a rough time for all of us. Just don't forget how much I care about you."

Carter

The moment Carter saw his daughter chatting with Toby, he took the opportunity to hightail it up the property line of the alpaca farm. Weezer still loved the funny-looking creatures, and Brooklyn and Caleb didn't mind her feeding them as long she didn't let them onto the winery.

Which would be bad right before harvest.

An alpaca named Alpachino had a thing for grapes and he once nearly destroyed a row of vines.

Weezer had texted her location. She hadn't spoken much to TJ since he'd run out of the winery. But she had brought him snacks to feed the alpacas and currently, there were six of them sticking their heads through the fence.

"Hey, honey," Carter said quietly.

"Sounds like you had quite a day."

"That's an understatement." He leaned against a tree about twenty feet from where TJ made friends with Lucy, of all creatures.

She was not the most friendly.

And she was a screamer.

But currently, she was calm and enjoying a head scratch.

Weird.

"How's the boy doing?" Carter asked.

"He's quiet," Weezer said. "Caleb was out, and TJ asked him questions about the alpacas' names and such. But other than that, I've been making sure the kid doesn't bolt."

"Why don't you give me a few minutes with him before Toby heads up here."

"I can do that." Weezer nodded. "I'll see you at home."

Carter rolled his neck. It had been a long time since he had to deal with teenage boys and while he's had to deal with a fair amount of drama in his family, especially when it came to Riesling and her ex, nothing compared to this. "Hey, TJ."

"Hi, Mr. River."

"Here at the winery, you can call me Carter."

"Yes, sir." TJ turned and took a seat on a large rock by the fence. "I take it my dad is back."

"He should be up here shortly, but I wanted a chance to speak to you alone for a moment."

"Am I in trouble?"

"No. Not at all," Carter said.

TJ's eyes filled with tears. "I knew my mom was up to something. She told me it was going to be good for her and that she wouldn't be going to jail. I didn't want that to happen."

"Neither did your father."

"That's what he said. But he also thinks my mom needed to have some kind of punishment for the laws she broke."

Carter sat down on a log across from TJ. "That part is over and your mom certainly did pay a price for what she did. But that's not what I wanted to chat with you about." He ran his hands across his thighs. He had to be careful what he said to TJ because he was Toby's attorney. He couldn't taint the boy's opinions one way or the other. "First, I want you to consider the winery a safe space. You can come here anytime you want, as long as your dad knows you're coming."

"Am I still going to live with my dad?"

Boy, nothing like jumping right in with the tough questions. "There is no reason to believe that will change."

"Will I still be able to do the summer hockey program and go to school at CWF Prep?"

"I don't see why not."

"What if my biological father and mom move? What if they want to take me somewhere else?" TJ's voice shook.

Poor kid. His mind had to be going a mile a minute.

"Do you mind if I ask you a question before we tackle that one?" Carter asked.

TJ shook his head.

"How do you feel about what your mom announced today?"

"I don't know." TJ swiped his eyes. "I always knew my dad adopted me. He's never lied to me about that and honestly, he's made me feel like I was special because of it."

Carter smiled. Toby might have had his faults, but when it came to being a good parent, he was hands down one of the best. Even when he went a little nuts at the ice rink, he did always have TJ's best interests at heart. "You are special, TJ. Don't let anyone ever tell you otherwise."

"My mom was texting me all day about some big surprise. I guess I didn't think she'd tell the entire world who my biological father was at the same time she told me." More tears. They were silent, but they still came.

Carter moved closer, kneeling in front of the boy, who had the height of a man. He couldn't say one single negative word about Serena. Or Brooks. All he could do was try to comfort TJ. "I'm sure that came as a shock."

TJ blinked. "Did you know that Coach Halsteder wanted Dax's job?"

"I did."

"And that he was at the rink the day my mom was arrested."

"I'm aware."

"Why didn't he or my mom tell me then? Or shortly after? Why did they wait until today?" TJ asked. "I know my mom will say it's because she hasn't seen me alone, but she's texted me. She's sent me emails. It doesn't make sense."

Oh boy. This might have been a mistake. Carter took TJ's hands. "Because I'm your father's lawyer, I can't say things that could be considered putting ideas in your head."

"Trust me. They are already there. A million of them. And they aren't good ideas. About anyone. That includes my dad."

At least the kid was opening up. "Listen. You have a therapist. That's a good person to talk to. My daughter Riesling and her husband Trey are also good people for you to talk to and you can also trust Zinny."

"But she's my dad's girlfriend. I know they haven't come out and told people that; however, I'm not stupid."

Charter chuckled. "No, you are not and it's true.

They are in a relationship, but you can trust Zinny. If you don't want her to tell your father something, she won't. Not unless it's something that is dangerous for you or something that is inappropriate for you to be doing." Carter squeezed the boy's hands before he rocked back to the log he'd been sitting on before. "Another person you can confide in is Weezer."

TJ smiled. "I don't understand why everyone in this town is so afraid of her. Every time I've been around her, she's been so nice and she calmed Lucy down. That alpaca came running toward the fence, screaming like I was about to kill the lot of them."

"Lucy makes a lot of noise."

TJ nodded in agreement. "My grandma once told me that the Weezer got away with murder and we always walked on the other side of the street when we saw her."

Carter tossed back his head and laughed. Hard. He'd noticed that every time Alice Weatherby was in town. She also had a tendency to change her hair appointments if Weezer was in the salon at the same time. He thought it was simply because Alice thought she was too good to breathe the same air.

Not because she thought Weezer had actually used that shotgun.

"Well, I can tell you that my Weezer has never hurt a soul."

"Now that I know her better, I believe that."

"Good," Carter said.

"Can I ask you something?" TJ asked.

"You can always ask me anything. I won't lie to you, but there are things I can't tell you or discuss with you."

"Wow. I don't know too many adults who will be that honest," TJ said.

"I see no point in lying. You're at that weird age where you're not a child, but you're not an adult either, yet you're being forced to deal with a lot of things that someone your age shouldn't have to. I'm put in a position where my job is to make sure you stay with your dad. I won't lie to you about that, which means I might not always have nice things to say about your mom when I'm in court. But I want you to understand I don't play dirty. I won't say or do anything that isn't true." Carter ran a hand over his chin. "Do you understand what I'm saying?"

"Basically, if you say something crappy about my mom, it's the truth."

"You're really a smart kid," Carter said. "I wish things were different and this divorce came down to shared custody. But it doesn't."

TJ nodded. "Do you know Brooks Halsteder?"

"I don't, but Dax does, and I suppose you could google him." Carter figured the kid really didn't need any prodding from him and there wasn't anything too horrible about Brooks on the internet. "But I wouldn't do that without someone sitting next to you."

"Why not? Is there something bad out there?"

"Not that I know of, but I think when you go searching for information about your birth father, it might be good to have someone you trust with you in case you have emotions about it that you need to talk about. Or if you just have questions."

"I take it that person can't be you."

"I wish it could be me. But what you have to understand is that I could be accused of trying to cloud your opinions of people in favor of your dad," Carter said. "You're going to be asked a lot of tough questions and the best thing you can do for yourself is to be honest."

"Even if it could hurt someone?"

"That's just it, son. Lying is the only thing that can truly cause those you love problems. Even if you think the truth is bad, just tell it. Trust me when I say secrets and lies will destroy everything."

"Can I be honest with you?"

Carter nodded.

"I want to stay at CWF Prep and I want to live with my dad."

"Then you tell that to the attorney the judge will appoint for you, along with your therapist." Carter leaned over and squeezed the boy's shoulder. "You don't engage your mom, or even your dad, in all the bullshit. If you need a safe place to land, you call Weezer and you can come here. Or you call Dax. You hear me?"

"Yes, sir."

Carter glanced over his shoulder. "Here comes your

dad." He stood. "You can tell your dad anything we talked about. That's fair. However, I won't ever repeat our discussions. You can trust that."

"Thank you."

Carter nodded. "I'll see you soon." He turned on his heel and headed down the path, pausing when he was only a few feet from Toby. "You've got a great kid in TJ. He's handling this better than you think."

"He stormed out."

Carter stole a quick glance at TJ to make sure he wasn't paying any attention.

TJ had gone back to the alpacas, feeding them the last of the treats Weezer had brought.

"Because he's hurting and he's being torn in two by his mother. I told him he has a safe haven here at the winery and with my family, but I made it clear that I can't be his sounding board. But you know, Zinny can."

"Are you serious?"

"I am. Just because Serena is trying to make you look bad by using my daughter doesn't mean TJ can't trust her with his feelings. But we can discuss that when he's not in earshot," Carter whispered. "Let's regroup in my office tomorrow when he's at school."

"I'm inclined not to make him go if he doesn't want to."

"That's fair, but I'd push to keep his life normal." Carter didn't want to tell Toby how to parent. It wasn't his call and he certainly didn't want to judge. However, he knew how things looked in the courtroom and in the court of public opinion. For the first few weeks, they were going to lose the latter battle. Carter was prepared for that. He'd been doing it for as long as he'd been in love with Weezer. However, he'd also been winning it for that long because he'd learned not to play the game the way everyone expected. He waited it out and by doing so, people soon realized he and Weezer and their family were just like everyone else.

Well, most people had.

The rest were the Serenas of the world.

"You think I should make him go?"

"I'd encourage it under the caveat he can have someone come get him if things get rough, because you do have a job and need an income."

"Good point."

"Not to mention it shows how much you care about his education."

Toby tilted his head. "I'm not doing any of this for show—"

Carter held up his hand. "I'm not saying that you are. But you have to understand that from here on out, this is a war. Serena drew the battle lines, and my job is to make sure you win." He pointed his finger toward TJ. "That he wins. The two of you belong together."

10

ZINNY

Zinny looped her arm through her mother's and strolled down Main Street. Growing up, like all her siblings, it had been a struggle to be Weezer's child, but for different reasons. Being the youngest allowed Zinny to watch her siblings' responses to their mother's outrageous antics and she'd learned that her mom did things for three reasons.

The first one was to get people to take action.

The second was to make sure people were listening.

But the last one was the most important when it came to understanding the Weezer's motivations and that was she did crazy things oftentimes to keep people at a safe distance.

That included her family.

Now, the older her mom got, the calmer she'd become because all the secrets were out. The fact her ancestors stole the winery no longer mattered and the doctor's secrets that were buried on the property have been discovered.

There was nothing left to threaten the Weezer or her family so she didn't have to act as crazy.

Just a little.

Zinny had to admit, she missed the wild and outrageous Weezer, but not so much that she was going to poke that bear.

"Are you ready for this interview?" her mom asked.

"Not much to it," Zinny said. "I just have to be honest."

"The entire thing makes me nervous." Her mom paused in front of the Green Bean. "I need a coffee. Do you want anything?"

Zinny waggled her brows. "Strawberry mocha—"

"I'll just go ask for the Zinfandel special."

Zinny laughed. It was true. The people who worked at the coffee shop had named the drink after her because she used to order like three a day. Now she was down to one, except lately.

This whole thing with Toby and being accused of abuse was getting under her skin. She was happy to go in and be interviewed by the police and the social worker. She understood it was more of a formality. But it still didn't settle right in her gut. Toby had never laid a hand on his son.

Ever.

He wasn't a violent man.

"And get me a chocolate muffin," she yelled to her mom.

Her mother waved her hand over her head before she disappeared inside.

Zinny sighed and sat down on the bench. She lifted her gaze. "Shit." She made eye contact with Serena of all fucking people.

"Well, well, well. Look at what we have here." Serena flipped her newly styled hair over her shoulder and clicked her heels across the pavement before plopping her ass right next to Zinny.

If she wasn't waiting for her mother, she'd get up and leave.

She should just get up and go wait for her mom by the door, but her muscles froze and she couldn't move.

"Cat got your tongue?" Serena asked.

"No. I've just got nothing to say to you." Zinny inhaled through her nose and exhaled slowly. Her dad always told her to focus on her breathing when she wanted to run her mouth.

It usually worked.

The key word there was usually.

If she had her drink, she could suck on the straw. That worked better because it gave her mouth something to do other than yapping.

"How about you listen then." Serena shifted, leaning closer. "Toby is going to lose and do you know why? I'll tell you why. Because he's a bottom-feeder.

He's never been truly successful at anything. He's always had to step on other people to get somewhere and—"

"Serena, I think you have Toby and yourself confused."

"You think you're all grown-up and smart, don't you."

"I did put on my big girl panties today," Zinny said.

"When this is all over." Serena inched closer. "You're not going to know what hit you, little girl." She stood, smoothed down her slacks, and strolled off like she was walking the runway.

Fucking bitch.

Zinny blew out a puff of air and squared her shoulders. No way would she let that woman rattle her. Not today.

Not ever.

She was a River. She was strong. And she was going to help Toby and TJ get through this.

Digging into her purse, she found her cell.

No texts from Toby.

They'd barely spoken in the last couple of days. Zinny did her best to understand that Toby was doing exactly what he needed to in order to take care of his son. That meant he worked, spent time with TJ, and strategized with her dad, leaving almost no time for her.

They had stolen kisses.

A few walks in the vineyard.

But that was it and she was not only feeling neglected, but cast aside.

Her mother stepped from the coffee shop and handed Zinny her drink. "No chocolate muffins left, so I got you a chocolate cookie."

"Next best thing." But she'd lost her appetite. Perhaps it would come back after this damn interview. She fell into step with her mom as they headed toward the courthouse. She shoved the straw in her mouth and sucked. The sweet drink filled her mouth and she moaned. "Thanks for coming with me."

"I wish this wasn't happening," her mom said. "It's crazy that you even need to answer questions about this."

"Dad said he was surprised that this was being dragged out. He asked Levi about it and all he said was that they were being thorough so it didn't come back and bite them in the ass."

"Your father told me last night he appreciates that; however, he's also concerned that maybe the other side is playing games."

Ha. Zinny knew that to be true. But there was nothing she, or anyone else for that matter, could do about it. Serena was a master manipulator and for years she'd gotten away with it. Riesling told Zinny that people like that eventually got so bold it all blew up in their face.

Well, that couldn't happen soon enough in this case.

The closer they got to the courthouse, the more her stomach twisted into knots. For the most part, Zinny had been a fearless kid. She went through her young life doing and saying whatever she wanted and never much concerned herself with the consequences. Of course, she never did anything illegal or shit that would get her into too much trouble.

She wasn't an idiot.

And she did think things through.

Her mom paused at the base of the steps and turned. She fiddled with Zinny's hair. "I don't tell you this enough, if at all. But I'm so proud of you, Zinfandel. You've grown into an intelligent, beautiful woman."

Zinny smiled. "Thanks, Ma." She leaned in and kissed her mom's cheek. "I better get inside."

"I'll be sitting right on these steps waiting."

"You don't have to. I'm a big girl."

"I know you are. But I want to."

Zinny wasn't about to argue with her mother. Besides, she had been enjoying her company. She turned and headed up the steps all the while taking in deep, controlled breaths. She had nothing to hide.

Her cell buzzed.

She dug into her purse and her heart fluttered. Her eyes burned.

Toby: *Thinking about you. :)*

Zinny: *I'll call you in a bit. Kisses.*

She dropped her cell back in her bag and headed inside with a new sense of strength. However, she'd forgotten how intimidating this place could be. Her father brought each of his kids down to sit in the back of a courtroom on a random day so they could watch the law in action.

Or really, watch criminals go to jail.

The sole purpose of that exercise was to scare the shit out of kids so they wouldn't do stupid shit.

Though, later, they each learned there had been nothing random about the time or the day.

She made her way to the designated room where the interview was to take place.

A social worker.

A judge.

And a police officer.

The receptionist for the judge assigned to the custody case led Zinny to a small conference room where she waited for a few minutes before a big door opened.

Judge Joyce Randall stepped in. She wore black slacks and a white blouse. She smiled and took a seat at the head of the table. "You must be Zinfandel River."

"Yes, Your Honor."

"I'd like to keep things a bit informal if we may, so you can just call me Judge, okay?"

"Yes, ma'am." Zinny wished two things. First, that

she hadn't drank all of her fruity beverage. And second, that she hadn't loaded herself up with so much caffeine.

"Or that," the judge said with a slight laugh. "I've had your dad in my courtroom a few times. He's an excellent lawyer."

"I've heard that about him."

"So, let me tell you how this is going to work." Judge leaned forward, clasping her hands together. "Because this is not the conventional way of doing this."

"I understand."

"A police officer is going to come in and ask you questions about two completely different situations. One of which you are potentially the victim and the other you are the witness."

"Yes. I'm aware." Her father had prepped her a bit. He also told her that the reason the judge was getting involved was because she wanted to understand why the sexual assault charges were constantly being brought up with Zinny when she herself had adamantly denied anything happened.

"So, you understand that as the judge on the custody case for TJ Tillman, I reserve the right to also question any potential witnesses and their credibility and because Toby was accused of abusing his son, if he had a past history of violence against children, well, it would stand to reason he might repeat that pattern."

"I understand, Your Honor." Her dad had coached

her to be respectful. If that meant calling Joyce Randall Your Honor or Judge, then that's what it meant. But she also carried with her a set of her own documents that proved two of the alleged allegations against Toby when it came to TJ were false.

And she knew without a doubt Toby had never done anything to hurt her—ever.

"Good." The judge picked up the phone receiver from the center of the table. "You can send in Officer Bob."

At least that was a friendly face.

Bob Cole had been an officer with the Candlewood Falls Police Department for as long as Zinny could remember. He wasn't always the most pleasant man, but he took his job seriously.

Sometimes, when it came to teenagers, maybe a little too seriously as he was the one who picked up the twins for streaking through town.

Even her dad thought that was hilarious and that they didn't deserve anything but maybe a slap on the wrist by their parents.

Not community service.

But he didn't complain since there was no permanent record to deal with and the boys learned that when you take your clothes off, there might be consequences.

However, to this day, the twins didn't care. As a matter of fact, there was a picture that made it to the front page. Their unmentionables were blurred out, but both of them had it framed and it was hanging in their apartment over their sofa.

Talk about immature.

A second door on the other side of the room opened and in strolled Officer Bob. He puffed out his chest, all cop-like. "Good morning, Judge," he said.

"Bob." The judge nodded. "I believe you know Zinfandel River."

"I do," Officer Bob said. "I'm sorry we have to see each other under these circumstances."

"It's okay," she said.

Officer Bob took a seat directly across from her and smiled. It appeared genuine. He set a folder on the table and opened it. He tapped his pen, engaging it. "Do you mind if we get right down to business?"

"Sure," Zinny said. Her heart beat so fast she thought she might choke on her own pulse.

"I want to start with the allegations that Mr. Toby Tillman sexual assaulted you."

"That's easy. He did not," Zinny said, holding Officer Bob's stare.

"Why would Serena Tillman say he did?" Officer Bob asked.

"I can only speculate and my father taught me that's a dangerous thing to do." Zinny wanted to say a few things, but opted to follow her dad's advice. This was his area of expertise and he kept telling her that sometimes, less was more.

Answer the questions and don't be too cute.

But be herself.

Which meant she had to toss in a few zingers.

"Okay." Officer Bob flipped a page. "Serena has told us that she saw Toby fondle you as a teenager."

"That never happened." Zinny sat up taller.

"She said that you were protecting him now because you're in a relationship with him," Officer Bob said.

Zinny had known the topic of their relationship would come up, but it still bothered her that she had to answer the questions. "I'm not protecting him."

"But are you in a relationship with him currently?" the judge asked.

"Yes. I am." Zinny hadn't meant to sound so proud of that fact, but she was. Okay. Maybe proud wasn't the right word. Thrilled? Ecstatic? Over the moon?

"For how long?" The judge had her own notebook and she scribbled away.

"About six weeks now," Zinny said.

"And nothing before then?" The judge stared at her with an intense glare.

"No, ma'am."

"Officer Bob," the judge said. "I think we can put to rest the sexual assault charges against Toby Tillman."

"Agreed, Judge. There just isn't enough evidence nor a victim." Officer Bob flipped over a few pages. "That brings us to the child abuse allegations."

The judge lifted the receiver again. "Can you please send in Brenda Cavanaugh?"

Zinny had heard the name, but only through Toby and only as the social worker assigned to the case. She'd come out to the house and she'd already spoken to Toby as well as TJ.

Toby had been rattled.

Zinny's dad told him not to worry, but now that Zinny was sitting in the hot seat, she was panicking a little.

A woman not much older than Zinny appeared. She had a folder, a little thicker than the one Officer Bob carried, and she set it on the table before taking a seat next to the judge. "Good morning," she said. "My name is Brenda."

"It's nice to meet you," Zinny said.

"Feel free to dive right in." The judge waved her hand.

Zinny swallowed. The reality of what was happening hit her right in the center of her chest. She concentrated on her breathing. In and out. Slowly.

"So, how long have you known TJ?" Brenda kept her focus on her papers.

"Most of his life," Zinny said. "I've been babysitting for him since he was a toddler."

"He speaks highly of you." Brenda nodded. "He said you're the one who took him to the hospital when he broke his wrist."

"I did." Zinny lifted her purse. "I actually have the speeding ticket that Officer Bob gave me that day."

Bob laughed. "I remember you tried to talk your

way out of it. You've certainly got your dad's gift of gab."

"It didn't work that day," she mumbled.

"I appreciate that. But I want to know what happened. In your own words," Brenda said.

"It's pretty simple." Zinny exhaled. "He was rollerblading in the driveway. He fell and landed on his wrist. It broke. It was an accident."

"Okay. What about the incident with the stitches?" Brenda asked.

"I don't know. I wasn't there. I can only tell you what I was told."

Brenda glanced up. "Okay. And the black eye?"

"TJ got into a fight at the rink. I saw the entire thing. I'm the one who told Serena and his father about it. I also filed the incident report at the rink. I brought it." She pulled it out of her purse.

"There was an incident report?" Brenda took it in her hands. "Thank you for this."

"You're welcome," Zinny said.

"Did you ever see Toby belittle his son at the rink? Call him names? Tell him he sucked at hockey? Or that he was worthless?" Brenda asked.

"No," Zinny said. "He was tough on TJ sometimes."

"Tough? How?" the judge asked.

"He expected him to have a good work ethic. To show up. To try his hardest," Zinny said.

"And if TJ fell short?" the judge asked.

"Toby would take his phone away. Or ground him.

Or he might not let him go to the movies." Zinny hoped this wasn't too much information.

"What about Serena?" the judge asked.

Oh shit. Her dad had warned her about sounding like the other woman. It was a fine line she had to walk when talking about Serena. She couldn't lie, but she had to choose her words carefully or risk sounding like she had it out for Serena and that wouldn't do Toby any good.

"She could be extremely tough on TJ," Zinny said.

"How so?" the judge asked.

"She and Toby had different parenting styles." Zinny wiggled in her seat. A bead of sweat broke out on her forehead. The air-conditioning did nothing to cool her down.

"Did she ever strike TJ?" the judge asked.

"Oh. No. I don't believe so." Zinny tried to keep her emotions in check. Serena was a lot of things, but she'd never seen her physically hurt TJ.

"What about emotionally?" the judge asked. "Did Serena ever hurt her son that way?"

Zinny's gaze shifted from the judge to Brenda, as if the young woman could save her from this line of questioning.

However, Brenda leaned forward and rested her hands over the top of her papers. "I'd like to know your thoughts on this as well."

Zinny's heart thumped right out of her throat. She tried to swallow but that became impossible. She wanted to run. Or hide under a rock. "I'm not a thera-pist. I sell wine for a living. I wouldn't know about this kind of stuff."

The judge tilted her head. "This is a custody case that is going to go to court because one party won't have it any other way. Because of that, I want to hear what all parties have to say. Because you are in a rela-tionship with the father, your opinion matters to me."

"No offense, Judge. But I'm not an expert and one thing I've learned from my lawyer father is that those are the only opinions that make a difference in a court of law."

"To a certain extent, your dad is right." The judge nodded.

"We're trying to do what's best for this young man," Brenda added. "What people see around them is important. What you see going on around TJ does matter."

"I'm sure I don't have to tell you that my sister, Chablis, was directly affected by what Serena and her mother did that led to their arrest," Zinny started.

"We're all aware of that," Brenda said.

"Then you have to understand that my opinion is incredibly tainted."

"That's about as honest an answer as one could ask for," the judge said. "But I still want to hear your thoughts."

Shit. This sucked. "In that case, I believe TJ should

be with Toby. Serena has proven that she puts herself above her family. Toby has never done that."

"So, you don't believe that being in a relationship with you is being selfish?" Brenda asked.

Ouch. That hurt.

"No. Because if it came down to me or TJ, I'd be gone," Zinny said. "But unless it's TJ telling Toby he doesn't want me in his life or our relationship is affecting TJ in such a way that's it's really hurting him, why should we break up? Because Serena wants us to? That's not the right reason. But I would walk away if I thought that was what was best for TJ. No one else. Just TJ."

"That's an interesting perspective. I want to thank you for taking the time." Brenda gathered her things. "I will have a report ready for you, Judge, by the end of the day."

"Thank you." The judge stood, shaking both Brenda's and Officer Bob's hands. She then waved toward the other door where she walked Zinny into the hallway. "It was lovely meeting you. Please tell your dad I look forward to hearing his arguments in my courtroom."

"I will do that." Zinny turned.

"Oh, and Zinny," the judge said.

"Yes."

"I expected you to be just like your mom, which you are in many ways, but you are also a lot like your dad."

Zinny smiled. "Thanks. I don't get that a lot." She

headed out of the courtroom feeling like she'd accomplished something good. The sexual assault charges had been dropped.

Hopefully, the allegations of abuse would be too.

Then it was on to the custody battle.

Let the mudslinging begin.

11

TOBY

Toby fiddled with the label of his beer. Some lovestruck female country singer belted her chops over the sound system at the brewery on the outskirts of town. The sound of a cue ball smacking into another ball rattled his ears. He'd left TJ with his mom so they could watch their favorite show together.

It had become a thing and it warmed Toby's heart that TJ enjoyed spending this time with his grandma. She wouldn't be around forever and the older TJ got, the more he'd be away from home.

Toby had hoped to be using this time to be with Zinny; however, that hadn't worked out as planned.

"You are in a mood." Dax straddled the bar stool as he sat down at the hightop.

"Zinny had her interview today," he said.

"Oh. How'd it go?"

"I have no idea. I haven't heard from her since she

left the courthouse." Toby glanced up. "I get that Eliza Jane went into active labor and she's at the hospital with her family, but I can't help it. I've got my feathers ruffled."

"Someone's got it bad for Zinny."

Toby wasn't going to deny it. Not with Dax anyway. But the rest of the yahoos who had shown up tonight, he'd prefer stayed in the dark. "Not the point. I'm concerned about what the judge thought and what happens next."

"Carter will—"

"He's at the hospital too," Toby interrupted, wishing he hadn't brought up the subject.

The waiter arrived with a plate full of appetizers and another round of beers. Toby had barely put a dent in his first one. His thoughts kept going back to Zinny.

She'd given him a few updates on Eliza Jane. The labor had been progressing nicely, though Toby cringed at the word. He couldn't imagine there was anything nice about labor.

Well, except maybe the end result of a baby.

Caleb, Brad, and Raf joined the table. These men had not really been his friends growing up. They had been Dax's and Malbec's, but they all had known each other and lately, they had been there for Toby when he really needed people in his corner.

"Is that Petra?" Dax asked, pointing to the bar.

"Yeah," Brad said.

"Who's that guy she's with?" Toby asked. "I don't think I know him."

"His name is Maverick. He's some cooking guru." Brad waved to Petra who smiled as she headed out the door with her takeout.

"If that's the case, why are they ordering food from this joint?" Dax asked.

"I didn't ask. I'm just glad to see her out and doing something." Brad shrugged before glancing at his watch. "Look, fellas, I've got maybe forty minutes left before I have to hightail it home. I've got a little lady and a bunch of kids to attend to."

"I never thought I'd hear those words come out of your mouth." Caleb slapped Brad on the back.

"I never thought we'd be sitting here with Dax and Toby and not have to break up a fight," Brad said.

"The night is young." Dax tossed a fry at Toby.

"Dude. You're skating on thin ice." Toby took an onion ring and flung it right at Dax's face. It felt good to let loose. He hadn't done this in months.

Actually, longer because he hadn't allowed himself to have real friends. Not during the last couple of years of his marriage. He realized he'd become ashamed of his life. Not his kid. Never of TJ.

But Toby hadn't liked himself for a long time and he didn't want people to know the real him because that person was ugly. Or at least he believed so until he started to fall for Zinny.

She helped him become the man he wished he

could be. The father he wanted to be for TJ. Without Zinny, he'd be a shell of a human.

"That's my line." Dax laughed as he lifted his phone. "Eliza Jane had a girl. Eight pounds, two ounces. Mom and baby are doing great. I guess Malbec had a bit of a meltdown, but otherwise, he's hanging tough."

"Please tell me she didn't name her Cabernet," Toby said as he pulled out his phone.

He had two texts from Zinny basically saying the same thing.

"You know she did. Cabernet Jane." Dax shook his head. "When Chablis and I have kids, we are not following that tradition."

"I don't blame you," Toby said. "I wouldn't either. Besides, there are only so many wines. You'd have to start branching out into something else."

"The other night, Ember and I were watching this documentary on bull riding," Raf said.

Dax burst out laughing. "Seriously. Why?"

"Why not?" Raf answered with a straight face. Sometimes Raf was a tough read. Talk about resting bitch face.

"Whatever floats your boat, man," Toby said.

"Anyway. They were talking about this guy, JW Whiskey. He holds the world record for bull riding. But his real name is Johnnie Walker. And he has three siblings. His sister is Georgia Moon and his baby brother is Jim Beam, but the funniest one is he has one brother his parents named Jack Daniel's, with the apostrophe *S* and everything."

"That borders on child abuse." Caleb laughed, but quickly cleared his throat. "I'm sorry. That wasn't funny."

"It would be if I wasn't getting ready to take my soon-to-be ex-wife to court." Toby raised his beer. "I mean seriously. She accused me of sexual assault of a minor and child abuse. Someday, I will be able to laugh at this."

"You have a great attitude, man," Caleb said. "Only way you're going to get through shit like this is to laugh a little and remember karma is a bitch and her name is Serena."

"I still can't believe the shit that she gets away with." Dax took a hearty swig of his beer. "Chablis and I really don't care what she did to us personally, but the fact that she has made it seem like she didn't do anything wrong pisses Chablis off."

"The tide is changing," Raf said. "People see Serena for who she is. No one believes this bullshit."

"But my son is paying the ultimate price." Toby pushed the empty beer bottle aside, opting not to have a second one. His stomach soured. "No matter how this plays out, that's his mother and he has to live with that fact. It's not like with Weezer, who is just a misunderstood character, and that's by design. My son has to live with this legacy for the rest of his life. Not to mention he now knows who his biological father is and while he's always known he was adopted, now he has a face to go with the rejection." Toby stood. "I'm really not good company tonight."

"Hey, man, we understand. Everyone at this table has been through some shit," Caleb said. "You don't have to apologize to us."

Dax reached out and curled his fingers around Toby's forearm. "Why don't we go to the hospital and see that baby together?"

Zinny would be there and that would be a sight for sore eyes and an aching heart since TJ was spending the night with his mom. Of course, Toby could stay there too if he wanted, but this was such a special treat for his mom. Why would he interject himself into that little party just because he was forty and lonely? "Okay." Toby dug into his pocket and tossed forty dollars on the table before taking his cell and tapping on Zinny's text messages.

Toby: *On way to hospital. Don't leave, ok?*

Zinny: *See you soon. Kisses.*

He smiled, running his fingers across the screen. It seemed so silly to get such a warm feeling from a single word.

Kisses.

But it reminded him that his life wasn't over. That when his divorce was final, which should happen in a couple of days, and custody was settled, he and Zinny could settle into whatever their future might look like.

He had no idea what was in store for them, but he looked forward to finding out.

"What put a smile on your face?" Dax gave him a nudge as they headed toward the parking lot.

"Nothing." He tucked his cell in his back pocket.

"Right." Dax laughed. "You and Zinny make for a sweet couple."

"She's a special woman." Toby hit the button on his key fob to his truck. "Thanks for tonight. For both getting me out with the guys and for reading my mood."

"My pleasure," Dax said. "What are friends for?"

"Listen. I might be asking some favors that I don't have the right to when it comes to TJ this summer and the coming year."

Dax held up his hand and shook his head. "Don't think twice. I'm his coach and he's a good kid. I want to see him succeed. So, whatever you need, just let me know."

Toby nodded. "See you at the hospital." He climbed behind the steering wheel. He didn't know what he did to deserve this turn of good luck, but he wasn't about to question it. He needed all the help he could get. The next week was going to be hell.

Toby

Toby made his way down the hallway toward Eliza Jane's room where he'd been told Zinny was visiting with her new niece. There were only so many visitors allowed at once and the rest of the family was in the waiting room, but told Toby to go ahead and join his girlfriend.

Girlfriend.

He was finally getting used to the idea.

Though his mother had strong opinions about it. She liked Zinny, but worried about the age difference and what people would think.

TJ had told his grandmother that he was okay with Zinny. That he thought she was cool. However, the second Toby's grandma mentioned Serena and asked what her thoughts were, TJ's face hardened.

The poor kid was caught between a rock and a hard place.

Toby had told his son not to worry about Serena, and then TJ fired back, asking about Brooks and how Toby felt about him. Well, that was a different situation, but Toby couldn't be a hypocrite. If Serena wanted to date Brooks, then so be it. But as long as Toby had custody, Brooks wasn't going to be in TJ's life.

The thing was, TJ had made it clear with his therapist that he didn't want to see Brooks. At least not yet anyway.

Toby rounded the corner and found Carter leaning against the doorjamb. "Good evening, sir."

"Hello, Toby. I heard you were here."

"News travels fast," Toby said.

"Weezer texted and told me I better cut my visit short so you could see the baby and visit with Zinny."

"Oh. I don't want to pull you from your grandchild. I just wanted to see Zinny for a little bit."

Carter shifted his stance, but still blocked the entryway. "I've just been standing here, watching Zinny hold that baby, and it reminds me of the day she was born."

"Having kids is a magical moment."

Carter nodded. "Grandkids are kind of fun too. I've got another one coming soon, and before I know it, I bet Chablis is pregnant."

"Your family is growing by leaps and bounds."

Carter turned. "I want you to know that I more than approve of you and Zinny. You're a good man and I can see that you care deeply for my daughter."

"I do, sir." Toby tried to control his pulse, but it was like a runaway bull.

"I didn't think my baby girl would be the next one to fall in love, get married, and have a bab—"

Toby coughed. "I'm not divorced yet, sir. And that conversation we had was just me thinking about..." Toby let his words trail off. His chest tightened as Carter shifted out of the doorway and Zinny came into view.

She sat on the edge of the bed holding baby Cabernet. Zinny's smile was as wide and as bright as the sun. Her green eyes twinkled like bright emeralds.

He'd never seen anything so stunning before.

"What were you saying, son?" Carter tapped him on the shoulder.

"Oh. That we're not ready to be..." But he couldn't finish the statement because his brain filled with ideas of what the future could bring.

Images of Zinny, her hair in a messy bun with little flowers in it, holding daisies and walking toward him filled his brain. He could see her with a round belly.

Or holding their child.

With TJ at their side.

It was as if he peered into a crystal ball and got a peek at what was on the other side of this insanity.

The happiness he was going to have.

He swallowed.

Hard.

"I can't believe I'm going to say this, but you're not too old," Carter said. "Have you told her you love her?"

"No, sir," Toby admitted. "The timing has never been right."

"If I had waited for the right time to tell Weezer I loved her the first time, we wouldn't be standing here." Carter squeezed Toby's shoulder. "The perfect time is the present."

Toby glanced between Zinny and her father.

"She's going to need a ride home," Carter said. "See you later." With that, he disappeared down the hall, leaving Toby there alone with all his feelings.

Zinny turned and smiled. "How long have you been standing there?"

"Just a few minutes." He inched closer. "Congratulations, Eliza Jane."

"Thanks." Eliza Jane waved her hand and smiled. "If Malbec were here, he'd be taking all the credit."

"But you did all the work." Toby laughed, leaning over Zinny's shoulder. "Oh. But she looks just like Malbec."

"I know. It's frightening," Eliza Jane said. "Let's just hope that as she grows up, she starts looking like Riesling because she and Malbec look the most alike and Weezer said they looked like twins as babies."

"I'm just glad Malbec isn't around to hear me say she's beautiful," Toby said.

"Do you want to hold her real quick before we get kicked out? Visiting hours are almost over." Zinny stood.

"Sure." Toby had never been a baby kind of guy until he had one. He used to hold TJ all the time and just stare at him, in awe that he'd come out of a human. That TJ was a real little person.

And that Toby got to be his father.

Toby believed that to be the highest honor, especially because TJ wasn't his biologically.

But he was his father in every way that counted.

Toby took Cabernet into his arms. He glanced at Zinny and smiled before easing into the chair next to the gurney. "She's a big one."

"Thanks for the reminder," Eliza Jane.

"TJ was only six pounds at birth." Toby thought he

might break the kid at first he was so tiny. "But he's making up for it now. I think he's going to be a few inches taller than me." He'd never cared about the genetics before, but knowing that Brooks could be in TJ's life, and TJ could see himself in Brooks, bothered Toby. It shouldn't. He always knew that someday TJ might want to know who his father was, and Toby and Serena had agreed they would tell him when he was old enough.

When he was an adult.

It just happened earlier than Toby had been prepared for.

"I can't get over how much she looks like Malbec," Toby said. "It's uncanny."

"No one is ever going to believe she came from my body." Eliza Jane yawned.

"We better let you get some sleep." Toby stood and placed Cabernet into the bassinet. "When baby sleeps, so does mommy."

"Thanks. And I appreciate you stopping by," Eliza Jane said. Her lids lowered over the center of her eyes.

Toby placed his hand on the small of Zinny's back. He guided her out of the room and into the hallway. "She'll be asleep in seconds."

"I bet that baby wakes her in ten minutes to feed."

"That's just mean." Toby laughed. "But probably true." He paused at the end of the corridor. He took Zinny by the forearms.

No time like the present.

"You want one of those, don't you?" he asked with his heart beating in the center of his throat.

"A baby? We've had this conversation."

"No. Actually, we haven't." He ran his thumb over her lower lip. She was so gorgeous. But it was her inner beauty that stole his heart and he'd never get it back. He hadn't known true love until he'd fallen for Zinny. "We danced around it, but having a family is important to you and I'm in love with you, so it's something we need to talk about."

Her jaw dropped.

She made this cute little noise that was a combination of a gasp and a screech.

"What did you just say?" she asked.

"That we need to discuss—"

She gently poked him in the arm. "Before that but after family is important."

"Oh. The I love you part." His heart filled his chest. He smiled like a big kid.

"Yeah," she whispered. Her long lashes fluttered over her crystal-green eyes. She gripped his biceps as if she were going to fall over. "That was an unexpected declaration."

"You father told me there was no—"

"Wait a second." She stuck her finger in her ear and wiggled it. "My father was privy to this before I was?"

"He asked me if I loved you. Was I supposed to lie to him?"

"No. He wouldn't have liked that."

He took her chin with his thumb and forefinger. "Zinny. Do you love me?"

"Well, duh. That's a dumb question."

"I don't know. We've been standing here discussing how your dad knows, but not whether or not you reciprocate and you haven't said it back. That's kind of important to me."

She raised up on her tiptoes and pressed her angel lips against his and kissed him hard. "Yes. I love you, Toby Tillman."

"Good," he said. "Now, back to this baby business and the fact that you want one, or two."

"Is this a problem?"

"I don't think so," he said. "I find myself wanting to give you everything your heart desires."

"First, I wouldn't want you to do something only for me. Having a baby is a we program. Second, it's a family affair. I'm a little old-fashioned when it comes these things."

"Are you proposing to me?"

"No. Especially not in a freaking hospital. I'm just saying I want the whole fairy tale."

"I get it." He kissed her nose. "And I want to be your Prince Charming. I want to do this with you. I want to have a family with you."

"Now that sounds like a proposal and my answer will be yes as soon as you do it up proper. That means asking my dad for my hand, making sure TJ is on board—"

He hushed her with a kiss. He didn't need her to tell him what to do. He knew her well enough to know she wanted to be swept off her feet. He'd seen that in her eyes with the small gesture Dax had done for Chablis.

"That shouldn't be allowed in a hospital hallway." Weezer's voice cut through his brain like a cattle prod.

He wasn't afraid of Zinny's mother, but there was nothing worse than getting caught in an intimate moment.

"That's a kiss meant for a hotel room," Weezer said.

His face flushed.

"Hi, Mother." Zinny dropped her head to his chest.

He wanted to take a step back, but his job now was to protect her and he suspected her cheeks were as bright as her hair was red.

"Hello, child," Weezer said. "Are you headed back to the waiting room?"

"I was going to take her home."

"Which one? Yours or hers?" Weezer asked. "I heard TJ was spending the night at your mom's."

Toby swallowed. "Mine," he said.

The sound of boots on the tile caught Toby's attention. "I think it would better if you stayed at the cottage tonight," Carter said as he rounded the corner. His voice was tight and harsh.

"Why?" Zinny turned. "What's going on, Daddy?"

"I just got an email from the judge." Carter waved his phone. "We have good news and bad news."

"Seems like that's the new theme of my life," Toby muttered.

"I'll start with the good. All charges have been dropped against you, as I believed they would be. The bad news is the judge wants to get this custody hearing started. Tomorrow."

"Why so fast?" Toby asked. "Is this typical?"

"The email I got from the judge stated that unless either party had a compelling reason not to begin, she wanted to make sure TJ's future was secure." Carter tucked his cell in his back pocket. "I can't say it's typical, but before these bogus allegations were tossed in your direction, custody was scheduled to be heard right after trial. I think the judge wants to keep things moving forward before Serena tries another crazy stunt."

"Is there a reason not to go to court tomorrow?" Toby asked.

"Well, the way I look at it, the longer we wait, the more of a chance Serena has to pull some more bullshit out of her ass." Carter lowered his chin. "I don't trust she doesn't already have something up her sleeve, so before we go to the courtroom tomorrow, I want to go over everything with you, and if you spend the night at Zinny's, we can start at breakfast."

"Sounds like a plan," Toby said. "What time would court begin and does TJ need to be there?"

"Opening statements start at one and no. But his lawyer will be. And he will be asked to speak with the judge, but she'll want to do that after school, so maybe Riesling can pick him up and bring him over. I suspect this will be a two-day custody hearing. I should have Serena's list of witnesses by eight tomorrow, if they agree to move this quickly."

"Are we really ready?" Toby asked. It had been a hot minute since they'd discussed the details of custody because they'd been so focused on the mudslinging.

"Nothing has changed. Our list of character references are the same. We have her conviction. The only thing that we didn't anticipate was Brooks. I'm still digging into his background. He's gotten away with some not so nice things, and he's been in a few fights. That will make any relationship he would have with TJ questionable."

"What about the fact he told Dax he didn't want to be TJ's father?" Toby asked.

"Dax will testify to that." Carter rested his hand on Toby's shoulder. "We've got a good case. Serena dug herself a bigger hole with her lies. Trust me."

"I do, sir."

"Okay. Stop with the sir, crap," Carter said. "It's Carter."

"Yes, sir. I mean Carter." Toby blew out a buff of air. "Thank you."

"Now get my daughter home safe and sound," Carter said.

"Don't do anything we wouldn't do." Weezer smiled.

Toby groaned.

"Have you told him how I got the nickname Weezer?"

"Mom. Really?" Zinny hugged her mother. "I wish I never heard that story. It's gross. It's embarrassing. No one wants to hear about their parents having sex. In public!"

"How on earth do you think you became you?" Carter laughed. "Though, with you, it was in the family bed."

"This is really my cue to leave." Toby took Zinny by the hand. "Good night, everyone."

"Make sure you use protection," Carter called. "Or not. Your call."

"You're not funny, Daddy." Zinny squeezed his hand. "Sorry about them."

"I guess if you and I are going to go the distance, I have to get used to this kind of razzing."

"That's probably a good guess."

"Okay then. Let's get you home and give them something to talk about."

12

———

TOBY

Toby raised his right hand and placed the other on the Bible as he swore to tell the whole truth and nothing but the truth.

It felt kind of strange to do so when there wasn't a jury. Everything would be decided by the family court judge.

Joyce Randall.

Carter had said she was a fair and reasonable woman, but that didn't make this process any easier.

So far, Toby had been incredibly impressed by Carter. His opening statement had been brilliant. He covered all the reasons why Toby should be given full custody. He didn't go into great detail why Serena was a bad mother, though he implied it.

Whereas Odette Moira spent her entire time bashing Toby, she didn't once have anything nice to say about Serena.

That seemed odd to Toby. As if the only way Serena could win was to prove Toby was a shit instead of showing she was the better parent.

Toby liked Carter's approach better.

They had listened to Dax's testimony as well as Chablis'. Both had been brief, and Odette, Serena's lawyer, hadn't had too many questions for them. Also taking the stand so far had been a couple of TJ's doctors and the school psychologist.

But Toby didn't know why he was taking the stand before Zinny. He understood that many of the character witnesses had made written statements to the court instead of testifying to save time, but Zinny was a huge witness. She'd been involved in all three of their lives for the last ten years.

"Good afternoon, Toby. Can you state your full name for the record?" Carter asked.

"Toby James Tillman."

"And how old are you?"

"Forty."

"So, you were twenty-six when your son was born, is that correct?"

"Yes, sir," Toby replied.

"TJ is not your biological son, is he?"

"No, sir. He's not. I adopted him."

"Was this at the urging of his mother?"

"It was my idea," Toby said. "When I proposed to Serena, I suggested that we become a family in every sense of the word."

"And did Serena have any objections?"

"No."

"What about TJ's biological father?"

"Serena contacted him, and he gave up his rights."

"So, you knew who he was," Carter said as a statement, not as a question.

"No, sir. I did not. Serena didn't want me to know and to be honest, neither did I. At that time, we decided that when TJ was an adult, if he wanted to know where he came from, we'd tell him, and then I'd learn that information as well."

"You mean to tell me that for fourteen years you didn't care where TJ came from? You weren't even a little curious? Or concerned?"

"TJ is my son. I love him. It doesn't matter to me what his biology is."

"When did you find out who TJ's biological father was?"

"The same time I found out Serena was having an affair with him," Toby said with a bit of shock that his voice didn't sound angry or hurt or have any malice laced to the words.

He felt nothing.

Not even hurt.

"When exactly was that?"

"A little over a year ago," Toby said.

"How did you find out?"

"I had left my laptop at work, so I asked Serena if I could use hers to log into my email. She must not have realized that she'd left her email open. I saw his email addy about three dozen times, so I clicked on an unopened one, and Brooks described in great detail the things he wanted to do to my wife."

"Objection, Your Honor." Odette pressed her hands on her desk and stood. "Besides the legalities of going into someone else's private email, even if the computer is open, and while we've seen this email since Mr. River was so kind to list it in discovery, it can't be proven that it wasn't doctored, and our experts couldn't find any trace of this exchange between my client and Mr. Halsteder."

"Your Honor." Carter turned and picked up something from his table. "While their experts might not have, we went to an independent source that the courts recommended, and they found the email chain in Serena's trash folder." Carter held up a stack of papers. "I just received them this morning and I have submitted them for your approval. I also sent them to the Miss Moira at eight this morning."

"Your Honor. This is absurd. I haven't had a chance to verify any of this. I strongly object," Odette said. "Besides, an affair doesn't have anything to do with whether or not my client is a good mother."

Toby hadn't known exactly what was in all those emails until this morning. He'd only seen the sexual stuff, which didn't make Serena a bad mom. It just made her a shitty wife.

"Your Honor. In these emails." Carter held up the papers. "Serena talks about how TJ is a burden and how she can't wait for him to be staying at CWF Prep full-time so that she and Brooks can begin their life together. But even before that, she often talks about how perhaps boarding school could be an option. These are time-stamped before their separation, before Serena's arrest, and before Brooks announced his paternity."

"I still object," Odette said.

"Overruled," the judge said. "I will allow the emails and the line of questioning."

"Thank you, Your Honor," Carter said.

Toby let his breath out. He hadn't realized he'd been holding it.

"How did you feel when you knew Serena was involved with TJ's biological father?"

"Betrayed," Toby said. "Scared. I still am afraid."

"Of what?"

"I understand that I adopted TJ, but you hear and read about all these stories of biological parents coming in and taking kids away from their families. How can I not be frightened of that," Toby said. He'd had his doubts about being honest about his emotions, but Carter told him to lay it all on the line. That he had a plan and to trust him.

"Has Brooks made any claim to TJ? Has he himself come out and said he wants to be a full-time—"

"Objection, Your Honor," Odette said. "Toby isn't

an attorney representing Mr. Halsteder. He wouldn't have any clue about what his intentions are."

"Overruled," the judge said. "I want to hear what Toby knows about the subject, and then I have a question."

"Thank you, Your Honor," Carter said. "Toby, please answer my question."

"I am not aware at this time that Brooks has taken any legal action to be in TJ's life," Toby said.

"Has he tried to see TJ? Call him? Contact him in anyway?" Carter asked.

"Not that I know of," Toby said.

"I'm curious about this too," the judge said. "I have not seen anything come across my desk regarding Mr. Halsteder and a request for visitation or even parental rights. I find that strange considering the stage we are in."

"May I approach the bench?" Odette asked.

"There is no jury in this case. Whatever you need to say or ask, just do it." The judge arched a brow.

"Yes, Your Honor," Odette said with a sigh. "Mr. Halsteder didn't feel that this was the right time. He wants to wait for custody between Serena and Toby to be settled before taking any drastic measures."

"Sounds like Mr. Halsteder is playing the odds to me," the judge said. "And if he really wanted to be a father, nothing would be stopping him."

Toby wished he could jump out of his seat and do

the happy dance, but he did his best to keep from smirking.

"Your Honor. My apologies, but that's not fair. You don't know what Mr. Halsteder is thinking," Odette said.

"You're right. I don't." The judge waved a piece of paper. "And since he's not on a witness list, I don't get to ask him, leaving me to wonder, and it's not making him or Mrs. Tillman look good. Now, Mr. River. Do you have any further questions?"

"Just a few more," Carter said. "Toby, why do you want TJ to go to Candlewood Falls Prep?"

"For starters, I went there," Toby said. "But mostly because TJ wants to."

"Are you sure about that?" Carter said.

"I can only go by what TJ tells me, and we've had many talks." Before tryouts, Toby pushed TJ hard, but once Serena left, Toby realized he might have been living a little bit too much through his kid. He decided to take a different approach and allowed TJ an out.

If he wanted it.

"TJ's pumped that Dax is going to be his coach and while he has some reservations about living on campus, he's told me that because of what is going on between me and his mom, right now, he'd rather live there."

"How does that make you feel?"

"Sad, but I understand, and TJ knows he can come home anytime he wants. That's the nice thing about him going to prep school in his hometown. He can also choose to live at home if he wants to."

"And you'd be open to that."

Toby smiled and sat up a little taller. "I'd love it."

"That's all I have, Your Honor." Carter nodded.

Now came the hard part and Toby knew it. Carter had warned him that he was going to leave the question wide open to where Odette could come in and question his relationship with Zinny. What Toby didn't understand was why didn't they nip that all in the bud.

Carter had explained that he'd circle back and clarify, but he hoped that Odette would go for the jugular and hang herself.

"The witness is all yours." The judge waved her hand to Odette.

"Thank you, Your Honor." Odette stood. "Mr. Tillman, are you currently dating?"

"I am."

"And who is the object of your affection?"

"Zinfandel River," Toby said.

"So, you're in a relationship with your lawyer's daughter," Odette said as a statement, not a question. "And how old is she?"

"Twenty-four."

"Tell me, Mr. Tillman. How old was Zinny when she started babysitting for you?"

"She started out as a helper. She might have been ten."

"So it's safe to say you've known Zinny for a long time," Odette said. "When did you start to develop feelings for her?"

"About the time Serena moved out," Toby said.

"Are you sure it's not when she was a teenager?"

"Objection, Your Honor," Carter said.

"Sustained," the judge said. "It has already been established that nothing has ever happened inappropriately between Zinfandel and Toby."

"All right," Odette said. "Mr. Tillman. Isn't it true that you once made a comment about Zinny's breasts and how she should be covering them up more when she was babysitting your son?"

"No. That was Serena, and she did it in front of everyone at our son's third birthday. As a matter of fact, I believe your uncle and his wife were there. They might remember." Toby cringed. He remembered that day well and he felt horrible for Zinny. She'd been maybe fifteen and just coming into her body. Serena shamed her something horrible and he worried it might scar her for life.

But not Zinny.

"Perhaps we should ask your uncle about that," the judge said.

Odette's cheeks turned red. "That won't be necessary."

"What does any of this have to do with Toby's ability to be a good father?" the judge asked.

"I'll move on." Odette lifted a folder from her desk and flipped through it. "Mr. Tillman, how many girlfriends have you had?"

"In my lifetime?" Toby asked.

"Sure." Odetta nodded.

"Not many. Serena. A couple of girls in college, and now Zinfandel."

"So, is it safe to say that no one else but Zinny would be sending you naked selfies?"

"Objection," Carter said. "What does sexting have to do with custody?"

Toby coughed, but he was impressed that Carter even knew the term.

"Your Honor. This goes to show Mr. Tillman's lack of awareness and how he's putting his sexual needs in front of his son," Odette said.

"I'll allow, but please make your point quickly," the judge said.

"Does Zinny send you naked pictures?" Odette asked.

"Objection," Carter said. "Your Honor. That's private and does not have anything to do with good or bad parenting."

"But, Your Honor, it does." Odette handed the judge a piece of paper. "These are the three phone numbers associated with the cellular account. Mr. Tillman does pay for this account, but what we need to note is that it's all attached to the same cloud account and that's how Mrs. Tillman found the naked pictures because they showed up in the shared family cloud. That their son sees."

"Your Honor, that's not true," Toby said.

"Are you calling me a liar?" Odette asked. "Are you saying these phone records are false? Are you trying to tell me these are not pictures that you and your girlfriend exchanged?"

Toby blew out a long breath and did his best to remain calm. He took the images and flipped them over so no one could see them. Especially Carter. "When Serena left—"

"Just answer the question with a yes or no, Mr. Tillman," Odette said.

"Your Honor, Miss Moira asked a series of questions. It's impossible for my client to do that."

"Agreed," the judge said. "Mr. Tillman, did you have something you wanted to say?"

"Yes. Thank you," Toby said. "I don't know how Serena got these because when she moved out, I got myself and TJ a new cellular plan, and I don't share cloud space with my son."

"Where do the pictures go, then?" the judge asked.

"They stay on my phone until I delete them, which I generally do pretty quickly," Toby said. "These are private. Meant to be shared between me and my girlfriend. I don't see anything wrong with them. I understand that they shouldn't be where my son can access them which is why Zinny and I are careful, so I'm confused on how anyone got them."

"So am I," Carter said.

"Do you have the records of changing phone companies?" the judge asked. "And how does Mrs. Tillman not know this?"

"Because I still pay her cell phone until Friday when our divorce is final. Then she will be responsible for her own phone bill. I was able to keep mine and TJ's number the same. I didn't tell her that I separated out the account. She does not have access to the new account."

"You're a smart man, Mr. Tillman," the judge said. "Miss Moira. I'd like to know how you were able to obtain these images."

"Um. Well, my client gave them to me through her cloud server," Odette said.

"Not good enough." The judge shook her head. "This will be stricken and I don't want to hear another word about this particular issue. I will be issuing a warrant to have this investigated further. I don't like the idea of someone's private images hacked and potentially shared in such a harmful way."

"Thank you, Your Honor," Carter said.

"Yes, Your Honor." Odette nodded. "Mr. Tillman. Isn't this entire custody battle because you're trying to get back at Serena because she left you?" Odette went right into her next beat.

"Absolutely not," Toby said.

"You're not out for revenge because Serena decided she wanted to be with TJ's biological father?"

"No," Toby said. "I don't want to hurt my son and trust me, that's exactly what this is doing. He doesn't want us fighting, but I can't allow Serena to continue to—"

Odette held up her hand. "Please. Just answer the questions. No need to give us a dissertation." Odette sighed. "I'm finished with this witness. His lies aren't getting me anywhere."

"Do you have anything else?" the judge asked Carter.

"No, ma'am."

"You may step down," the judge said.

Toby let out a long sigh as he made his way back to the table and his seat next to Carter.

"You did good. Real good," Carter said. "They've got nothing. And the fact that Brooks hasn't even filed for paternity speaks volumes."

"I'm so sorry about the pictures," Toby said softly. "It's not what you think."

"You have no idea what I'm thinking," Carter whispered. "Do you love my daughter?"

"Yes."

"Do you respect her?"

"Absolutely," Toby said with conviction.

"Then let's move on."

"Your Honor," Odette started. "We know that next on the list is Zinfandel River, testifying for Toby Tillman; however, we'd like to call her as a hostile witness."

"Excuse me." Carter stood. "What the hell for?"

Toby's heart dropped to his feet.

"Mind your tongue in my courtroom, Mr. River." The judge lowered her chin. "I don't begin to understand the antics where there isn't a jury in this case. But also, it doesn't matter what order the witnesses are called, so I will allow it."

Carter sighed as he sat down. "We knew they were going to come at this relationship. It's smoke and mirrors and it shouldn't affect custody, but I still don't like it."

"Zinny is tough. She can handle this."

"That's what I'm afraid of."

Carter

Carter knew two things for certain when it came to this custody case.

First, Toby had a real chance for full custody. His record was impeccable. He wasn't violent.

And he hadn't tried to manipulate the court or anyone else.

Where Serena had been all over the map.

Second, Odette was going to come hard after Toby's moralities and that meant using Zinny to do it.

Of all his children, Zinny had to be both the wildest and the most conservative. Most people couldn't understand that unless they knew her mother well. Weezer had always been the kind of woman who didn't like being told what to do, when to do it, or how to do something. If anyone dared, she tended to go the opposite way.

Unless it had to do with the winery.

That she always towed the line—to a fault.

Zinny was exactly the same way. He remembered when she'd been three years old and the preschool was putting on a little Disney musical. Zinny wanted to be Simba, but the school told her because she was a girl, she should play Nala. That didn't go over well, and she refused to even participate unless she could be a boy.

The school thought she'd come around. So did her teachers. Only, Weezer came in and told them if they didn't let her play a boy role, she'd take her kid out of that school.

Carter still found the entire thing hysterical, but from that moment on, Zinny wore only boy's clothes to school and it wasn't even Weezer's idea.

"Keep your cool," Carter whispered to Toby. "They are going to say a lot of things to try to rattle both of us. Don't let it."

"Yes, sir."

"I can't wait until this is over because I'm so sick and tired of you calling me that."

"Would Dad be better?"

Carter closed his eyes for a brief moment. "Are we that far into this relationship?"

"We are."

"That's the most interesting way anyone has ever asked me—no, informed me—they plan on marrying my daughter." Carter laughed. "We'll chat about this later."

"I was hoping that would get me off the hook."

"Oh, no. Not even close."

The doors in the back of the courtroom opened and in walked Zinny. She wore dark slacks with dark pumps and an ivory blouse. Her long red hair was styled in a wavy look that bounced over her shoulders. She had a touch of eyeshadow that brought out the green color and a tad of lipstick.

She was a natural beauty and Carter couldn't help but be a proud father.

He pushed a pad and pen in front of Toby. "If you have something you need me to comment on, or if you are upset over something, write it down. Don't scoff, sigh, or say a word."

"You really think they are going to try to make Zinny look bad?"

"I do," Carter said. "I just don't know exactly how or what they are going to bring up from her past."

Zinny swore on the Bible and took her seat. She smiled at Carter.

Or maybe it was Toby.

Could have been meant for both.

"Miss River," Odette said, holding a folder.

If that woman pulled out naked pictures, Carter was going to lose his shit.

"How long have you been sleeping with Mr. Tillman?" Odette asked.

Carter kept his gaze on the papers on his desk. He didn't want to either rattle his daughter or make her say something they all would regret.

"Since shortly after Serena was arrested."

"And how long have you had feelings for him?"

"About a year," Zinny admitted.

"Are you sure it's not longer?" Odette approached the witness-box. "Are you sure it didn't start when you were babysitting for Mr. and Mrs. Tillman when you were as young as twelve?" She flipped open the folder and held up a folder that had Zinny and Toby written on it surrounded by a heart.

Zinny laughed. "I'm sure."

"Isn't this yours?"

"It is," she said. "How did you get it? Did you break into my parents'—oh, wait. That must have come from when we cleaned out my dad's place and he moved back into the family house. Did you find the one that had me marrying the judge's oldest son? Because I had a crush on him too. Or how about the fire chief?"

Zinny fanned herself. "I think I had me marrying him and having three or four kids."

Carter covered his mouth and pretended to clear his throat. That was his Zinny.

"This isn't a joke," Odette said.

"I know. But I was a kid when I did that." She tapped her finger on the paper. "The fact that you only brought that one is funny. I had crushes on my teachers. On all sorts of male role models. It's normal. Heck. I have a folder with *I love Officer Bob* written all over it."

Everyone in the courtroom burst out laughing, including the judge.

Except for Odette. She didn't even crack a smile.

Leave it to his daughter to lighten the mood.

"Didn't you have at least one crush on an adult when you were a kid?" Zinny asked.

"I'm not fighting for custody of an innocent child. Nor am I in a relationship with someone who is sixteen years older than me."

"Your point?"

Oh, Zinny. Don't bait her. That's not going to be good.

Or maybe Zinny, of all people, could trip this chick up. Serena's custody claims weren't that solid. She had evidence to prove that Toby was unfit, and yet Toby's case was solid as a rock.

"This isn't the first time you've been involved with an older man who lost custody of his child, is it?"

Odetta planted her hands on her hips. "Didn't you break up with him because he had a child?"

"That's misleading. The man you're talking about gave up physical custody, but still has visitation." Zinny narrowed her eyes. "And that's not why I broke up with him."

"Why did you end that relationship?" Odette asked.

"That's none of your business," Zinny said.

"Answer the question," the judge ordered.

Shit. Carter had known about Levi, but he didn't know the details, other than Levi hadn't wanted to be a father. His ex-wife got pregnant and Levi dived into his work.

"Two reasons. He cared more about his work than he did his kid, and he didn't want to have more," Zinny said. "The latter was a deal breaker."

"All right." Odetta shuffled a few pages.

Carter had honestly started to wonder if Odette had anything of substance. Or why they thought calling Zinny first would do them any good. The naked selfies had backfired and the fact that Toby had bought himself and his son new phones under new a new account gave the judge reason to be concerned that Serena had obtained things illegally.

Serena was digging her own grave.

"Miss River, we know you have a thing for older men. You also like to send naked pictures of yourself."

Carter should stand up and object, but he wanted to see where this was going.

Toby poked him with the pen.

Carter ignored him for now.

"As the judge has pointed out, these are not illegal and while I personally find them distasteful and I wouldn't want my ex-husband's girlfriend—if she did these things—to be around my child, it's been made perfectly clear that as long as the child isn't being harmed or doesn't see the images, it's okay. However, what about having a man pay you for sex?"

"Excuse me?" Zinny jerked her head.

"Objection." Carter pressed his hands on the table and stood.

"I have here two affidavits from men who went to college with Zinny who paid her for sex. That's a crime."

"That's bullshit," Zinny said. "No one has ever paid me for sex."

"Are you sure about that?" Odette arched a brow.

"Yes. I am." Zinny folded her arms across her chest. "I think I would remember that."

"Your Honor. I only obtained these this morning." Odette handed a couple of papers to the judge. "Both gentlemen stated that Zinny required payment in the form of expensive jewelry. I have the receipts."

"Are these men named Rick and Joe?" Zinny asked.

"As a matter of fact, they are," Odette said. "So, you remember."

"Oh. I remember them okay, but you are completely misinformed."

"I don't think so." Odette handed the judge more paperwork. "I have sworn statements about all the sexual favors you performed. And where. And let me tell you, it reads like an erotic novel of sorts. Both Rick and Joe, however, couldn't afford your services for long. I wonder if we had more time and dug deeper, how many more young men we'd find."

"You wouldn't find any," Zinny said. "Because it's not true."

Carter closed his eyes and shook his head. This was meant to embarrass Zinny. Or him. Or both. But there was no point in objecting. Zinny was handling this just fine.

He glanced at Toby; thankfully, he held his head high.

Carter grabbed a piece of paper and a pen.

Are you okay? he wrote. *None of these things are true.*

Toby took the pen.

I know. But I'm both proud and mortified at the same time.

You'll get used to that feeling. It goes with being in love with Zinny, Carter wrote.

"Can you prove it?" Odette said.

Carter wrote, *Here's where you get to be really proud and see why I'm not objecting.*

"Um. Yes. I can," Zinny said. "You see, Rick was harassing me. It got so bad I had to file a restraining order at school. I believe my dad might still have a copy of it."

Carter stood. "I do, Your Honor. I also have copies

of all the expensive pieces of jewelry he bought to try to gain her affection along with the disturbing notes he sent my daughter. The harassment got so bad we filed suit. It was settled and sealed. Zinny was seventeen when she went to college, so you see, she was still a minor. That might be why Miss Moira didn't find it."

Odette cleared her throat. "That doesn't explain Joe."

"Joe is Rick's cousin." Zinny folded her arms. "It might be a good guess that he would take Rick's side and lie."

"Miss Moira. I would suggest that you do a better job of due diligence," the judge said. "Do you have any relevant questions for this witness?"

"I have just a couple more," Odette said. "Miss River. Have you ever seen Serena harm her son?"

"Physically? No. I have not," Zinny said. "But I haven't seen Toby do that either."

"Okay. Have you ever heard either of them belittle him? Call him names? Tell him he's not worthy of something?" Odette asked.

"Yes. Serena has done that, especially when it comes to hockey," Zinny said. "I've seen her tell TJ that he's not going to amount to much unless he does exactly what she says and not the coaches. Or his father for that matter."

"One final question." Odette pulled out a piece of paper. "Is this your letter to CWF Prep regarding Toby Tillman?"

Shit. Carter had forgotten all about that.

"Yes," Zinny said.

"And what does it say?" Odette asked.

"It's a plea to make sure that Toby and Serena aren't allowed in the arena during the showcase," Zinny said with a straight face and a whole lot of conviction. "I wrote it because at the time, I knew how Toby could get and with Dax Fabion coming back into town, I was worried that Toby would let Serena and her ideas get under his skin. And truth be told, I was right."

"What do you mean by that?" Odette asked.

"Dax and Toby have a history. They are good now, but during the showcase, which is when Serena left Toby, I was concerned that Toby would follow Serena's lead and take out his frustrations with Dax on TJ," Zinny said.

"And were you right?" the judge asked.

"I was wrong," Zinny said. "Toby kept his cool most of the time. He does expect a lot from TJ, but that's because TJ is really good. Ask Dax. He should know. He's an ex-NHL player."

"I'm aware of who he is," the judge said.

"The thing is, Your Honor, Toby was dealing with his wife cheating on him with the biological father of his son, and Dax coming back to town. It was a lot and I watched how it affected Toby and his confidence. It wasn't easy for me. I was falling for Toby long before anything happened between us. But even more than that, there was TJ. He was scared and confused and didn't understand what was going on." Zinny shifted in her seat, focusing on the judge.

Carter couldn't have been prouder of his baby girl.

While this wasn't in front of a jury or even a courtroom full of people and the media, her composure was top notch.

"Toby and Serena had asked me to help with getting TJ to and from the rink during this time. Actually, I had been helping with TJ for months at Serena's request. If I had known it was because she was having an affair—"

"You don't know that," Odette interrupted.

"But I do," Zinny said. "Her cheating on Toby doesn't really have any bearing on custody." She glanced toward her father. "I understand how the law works better than most. I grew up in what can be described as a broken home, but more importantly, my dad's a lawyer. Anyway, I can show you pictures I've taken on my phone of proof Serena was having an affair."

Toby scribbled on the notepad.

I didn't know she had proof. I don't know if I'm tickled pink or pissed.

"Because the divorce will be final this week and he didn't need them, I didn't feel the need to add insult to injury. TJ didn't need to know about the affair, even though I know he does. He certainly didn't need to hear that Serena had an on-again, off-again affair with Brooks for a few years, especially when Brooks is his biological father."

"Your Honor, I'd like to stop this right here," Odette said. "This is not helpful."

"Actually, I want to hear what Zinny has to say," the judge said. "Please continue."

"I know what it's like to live where everyone in town speculates. I'm lucky though; the majority of all that gossip is false. But I can understand how important it is to protect a child when the whispering might be true. Even though I would have loved for Serena to have a taste of her own medicine, outing her affair would have only hurt TJ."

"What about Toby? Didn't he have the right to know?" the judge asked.

Zinny glanced between the judge and where Toby sat. "I wanted to tell him, especially because I cared about him. But it still wasn't my place and it came out anyway before the showcase. Which, by the way, I was told they would only ask Toby and Serena to leave the rink if they misbehaved."

"Did you tell Toby what you did?" the judge asked.

"No, ma'am. This is the first he's hearing about it."

"I believe I've heard enough," the judge said.

"But Your Honor—"

"Please sit down," the judge interrupted Odette. "Miss River, you can take a seat. I will be speaking with TJ's lawyer as well as the social worker in this case in an hour. I will make my ruling in the morning. This court is adjourned."

Carter stood and faced Toby. "Are you okay?"

"Yes. And no."

"What's bothering you the most?"

"Do you really have to ask?" Toby said.

"She didn't tell you to protect your feelings."

"At first. But what about after Serena moved out and I confided in Zinny on why she left?" Toby asked. "I told only two people that she had an affair. Dax and Zinny. I'm sorry, Carter. I can't help but be angry. I can forgive a lot of things, but the fact she had proof and kept it from me all this time, I'm not so sure I can."

"I'm not telling you to squelch your emotions. I'm simply asking you to put yourself in her shoes for two minutes and try to see things from her point of view." Out of the corner of Carter's eyes, he saw Zinny approach.

This might not go over well.

She placed her hands on Toby's shoulders.

He shrugged them off.

Shit.

"Excuse me," Toby said. "I need some air." He made a beeline for the door.

"What the hell?" Zinny took one step, following Toby.

Carter took her by the arm. "Let him be, baby girl."

"What? Why? What the heck is wrong with him? I crushed it."

"You did," Carter said. "But you also never told him that you knew about Brooks and that hurt him."

"It would have hurt him more if I told him two years ago his wife was fucking the father—"

Carter covered his daughter's mouth. "Take a beat and think about that for a second. You're in love with him now and he loves you back. But back then, he still loved her and his family was all that mattered to him. You were the person who helped out with his boy. You were his friend. Your job was to be honest with him and you betrayed that trust. It doesn't matter if you did it to protect his feelings; you ended up hurting him anyway."

"Dad. I didn't tell Toby because I had feelings for him. I didn't want him to think I was using that information to seduce him or something. He was married and completely unavailable. Besides, it wasn't my business. Haven't you and Mom always told me to stay out of other people's relationships? That it's not our place to—"

"Okay. You made your point," Carter said. "To me. But Toby might feel differently. He also might want to know when you knew about Brooks."

"I know he knew about him before I did, but I'm guessing Toby is going to be mad that I knew at all and didn't tell him."

Carter nodded. "Oh, my sweet little girl who is normally wise beyond her years, but doesn't know the first thing about love."

"Yes, I do," Zinny said. "And I get that I made a mistake. I also know how to take care of it." She leaned in and kissed his cheek. "I don't need my dad to counsel me on that."

Carter pulled her in for a hug. "I suppose you don't. However, let me give you one piece of advice."

"What's that?"

"Don't come on too strong. Being in love with you is like being in the eye of a hurricane."

Zinny laughed. "Is that what Grandpa said to you about loving Mom?"

"No. He used a tornado analogy."

13

—————

ZINNY

Zinny knocked on the front door. She could have used her key, especially since she knew Toby was at home, but she decided that wasn't a good idea. Not considering he hadn't answered her text. Or her phone call.

But she wasn't going to be shut out.

He could be mad.

That was fair and reasonable.

But ignoring her?

Nope.

That wasn't going to fly.

He opened the door. "What are you doing here, Zinny?"

She planted her hands on her hips and jerked her head. "Seriously?"

"Yeah." He nodded.

"We need to talk." She took one step forward.

He blocked her way. "TJ is here."

"Okay. Come outside. This can't wait."

Toby stepped onto the front porch and closed the door. "This isn't the time or place."

"My dad told me things with TJ's lawyer and social worker went well," Zinny said, deciding that starting with a bit of small talk might be helpful. She strolled to the side of the porch and took a seat in one of the Adirondack chairs.

Toby sat down next to her and sighed. "I guess so."

"He's feeling really good about things."

"What do you want?" he asked, crossing his legs.

"To talk about why you're mad." She held his glare. One thing she knew about him is when he got pissed, he could hold on to that anger for a long time.

But she wasn't about to let him fester too long. As a matter of fact, she wouldn't allow it another second. She grew up in an environment where you got mad, you expressed it, and then you either got over it or you didn't.

Your choice.

Her family made too many mistakes in the latter.

"There isn't anything to chat about," Toby said. "You should have told me. Pure and simple."

"No, Toby, it's not. For all I knew at that time, you were madly in love with your wife and didn't want to know."

"I think every spouse wants to know if their partner is cheating on them."

"Okay. Perhaps that's true. But what you fail to understand are my feelings."

He turned and glared. "What does that mean?"

"I've cared about you for a while now. Longer than you've had feelings for me."

"Are we talking romantic emotions?"

She nodded. "When I learned about Brooks, I was already fantasizing about you and me and not like when I was twelve and I had a crush like I did on Officer Bob."

"He's not even cute," Toby said. "And I can't believe you said that in court."

"Focus on our problem." Zinny shook her head. "I thought about telling you that I knew, but what difference did it make?"

Toby reached out and took her hand. "It makes all the difference once we became an item." He kissed her palm. "I'm not mad that you didn't tell me when you found out. I'm upset that you didn't tell me once we slept together. Can you understand that?"

"Yes. And I'm sorry," she said. "I can't tell you how relieved I was when you found out the truth about Brooks."

"That was my next question," Toby said. "When did you know he was TJ's father?"

"About eight months ago," Zinny said. "But you knew before that."

He nodded. "Deep down I've always known who TJ's father was." He tugged her from her seat, pulling her to his lap. He kissed her neck. "I played Juniors for one year before going to play Division I college hockey. I didn't give Serena a second thought until I came back to Candlewood Falls, which was a little over a year before she returned. I hate to admit this, but I looked her up."

Zinny wanted to interrupt and ask a million questions.

But she opted to lean into his chest, wrap her arms around his shoulders, and listen.

Her father would be proud.

"I learned about her and Brooks." Toby inhaled and let it out with a whoosh. "I also found out about what happened between Brooks and Dax, but I was more focused on her and what appeared to be a really bad relationship, and my heart went out to her."

"You loved her in high school."

Toby chuckled. "How can you just say that and not be upset by that fact?"

"Because I love you and it's part of who you are," Zinny said. "Besides, I've known Serena a long time and even I can see she once had a good side. But somewhere she lost it and she's become a bad person. I'm sorry, but I do worry she'll end up hurting you or doing something that will hurt TJ."

"I agree. That's why I went all out in this custody battle. Otherwise, I would have agreed to joint. But I can't give her an inch. She'll end up pulling TJ from the things that he wants, though I worry maybe CWF Prep isn't the be-all and end-all for him."

"No. I think it is. And don't get mad or jealous, but Dax being the coach helps. Also, you being named assistant coach will be even more special."

"Wait. What?"

"Yeah. Don't tell Dax I let the cat out of the bag." She rested her head in the crook of his neck. "I shouldn't have told you, just like I probably shouldn't tell you that TJ has confided in me who he wants to live with."

"He told me too, but did you tell the judge that?"

"I wasn't asked," she said. "But the social worker did ask me and I did tell her."

"Why didn't you tell me?" Toby asked.

"In part because I felt like TJ told me in confidence." She lifted her gaze. "We both know Serena will get visitation. But I understand and agree it should be limited and controlled because she's manipulative. TJ knows that, but she's his mother. No matter what she's done —good, bad, or indifferent—he still loves her."

"I do know that," Toby said. "But I can't have her making decisions for him, or around him that much. And Brooks—shit—he doesn't want him, and I need to make sure he's not around. But that sucks for TJ. It's going to make him feel—"

"What am I going to feel, Dad?" TJ stood in the doorway. Tears streamed down his cheeks.

"Shit," Toby mumbled as he stood, lifting Zinny

right off his lap. "TJ. How long have you been standing there?"

"Dad. What are you worried I'm going to feel for Brooks?"

"I'm going to go inside," Zinny whispered.

"No, Zinny. Stay," TJ said.

Oh boy. This was going to be rough.

Toby

Toby's emotions were all over the place. He couldn't stay mad at Zinny if he tried. She'd done what she thought was best for TJ. Toby couldn't fault her for that.

Even in this moment, she continued to think about everyone else but herself.

Zinny was the most selfless person he'd ever met.

But he'd have to deal with all that later.

Right now, he was staring down at a confused and angry teenaged son.

"How much of that conversation did you hear?" Toby asked his son.

"Enough," TJ said in a grown-up voice. "What are you afraid I will feel?"

"Rejected," Toby admitted. "Abandoned. Unloved."

"Why do you care if that's what I feel by Brooks? I would think that's what you'd want," TJ said.

"Oh, my God. No." Toby closed the gap between him and his boy. He grabbed TJ by the biceps. "I might not like Brooks. And I certainly don't want him in your life. Not if I can have a say in it. But that doesn't mean I want you to feel bad about it, especially if Brooks had a genuine desire to be a part of your life."

"If he did, would you support that?" TJ asked.

"I would." Toby meant it, too. "I wish things were different with your mom as well. I want you to understand that there three reasons I'm fighting her over custody. The first one is what she did to Chablis. The second one is what she's done to our family. And finally because she's chosen to lie. I can't accept that."

TJ flung himself at Toby, wrapping his arms around his father.

At fourteen, TJ was a half an inch shorter and Toby stood at six feet. "I don't want to know Brooks and that makes me feel like I'm a bad person."

"No, kiddo. You're not bad. You're reacting to how he treats people." Toby hugged his boy tight. Tighter than he had in years.

He glanced over his shoulder.

Zinny sat in her chair. She swiped at her cheeks.

Toby gave her credit for sticking this out. Many women would have walked away a month ago. And tonight, they either wouldn't have shown up, or they would have left ten minutes ago.

"What if Mom gets custody? Or you have to share?" TJ asked.

Toby guided his son to the chairs and sat down. "Sharing wouldn't be horrible. Basically, your mom and I would have to agree on things, and I know that sounds impossible, but some of those things are already set in stone."

"Like what?" TJ asked.

"Like living in Candlewood Falls," Toby said. "Neither one of us could take you from your hometown. And we can't pull you from your school. That's all set in the divorce and custody papers, regardless."

"But what if Mom gets custody?" TJ asked. "Because she says she and Brooks are going to take me away from New Jersey."

"That's set in stone, like your dad said," Zinny said.

Toby appreciated Zinny's words, but he wasn't sure that was the case if the judge ruled completely in Serena's favor. Giving up control of TJ's well-being to Serena would be the most difficult thing ever. Toby prayed he never had to do it because if he did, he didn't think he'd ever survive.

It would be like ripping his heart out and stomping on it.

"I'd run away if I had to live with Mom and Brooks and I told the social worker that," TJ said.

"I'm glad you felt comfortable telling them how you felt," Toby said.

TJ stood and inched closer to the front door. "They

asked me what I thought of Zinny and how I felt about you dating her." TJ turned. "It would be okay with me if she stayed tonight and we had breakfast together in the morning before I went to school."

Toby sucked in a deep breath.

"Are you sure?" Zinny asked. "I don't mind sneaking out at two in the morning."

TJ laughed. "My dad bought chocolate chips so you better make those waffles I like."

"Oh, heck yes," Toby said. "I say it's a moral imperative that Zinny stay over just for chocolate chip waffles."

"And crispy bacon," TJ said. "You suck at breakfast food."

"Are you saying your dad is a bad cook?" Toby asked.

"If the apron fits." TJ waggled his eyebrows as he opened the door. "Good night, Zinny. Good night, Dad. I love you."

Toby tapped his chest. "Night, son. I love you too." He took Zinny's hand. "This is new territory for us."

"It sure is. I hope you have an extra toothbrush somewhere. I'll just take that Boston Bruins T-Shirt to sleep in."

"Absolutely not. You can wear one of my plain white shirts."

Zinny stood, laughing. "If you want any kind of treat tonight or in the morning, you'll give me the Bruins shirt. Otherwise, you'll be tossing and turning while I'll be completely in my birthday suit and the policy will be hands off."

"Oh. That's mean."

"Cough up the shirt and I'll be the nicest girl you've ever met."

Toby took her by the hand and tugged. "Fair enough. Let's go get naked."

14

———

TOBY

Toby slipped from the bed and took a moment to stare at Zinny. Her long red hair cascaded over her shoulders.

And his Boston Bruins T-shirt.

He knew he'd never get that back.

He sighed. He had to admit it looked good on her, only it had the entire team's autograph on it from when he got to drop the puck when he'd been only seven years old.

It had been the highlight of his entire hockey career.

Zinny's lashes fluttered. She shifted in the bed, pushing herself to a sitting position. "What time is it?"

"Five twenty," he said.

"I need a strawberry mocha—"

He laughed. "I don't have any way of making you that, so you'll have to wait until we head to the courthouse."

"Okay. Plain coffee then. But you better have some flavored creamer left."

"I have plenty." He bent over and kissed her sweet angel lips. "I'll go start a pot and make sure TJ is awake. I'll see you downstairs."

"Okay." She closed her eyes.

He turned and stepped out into the hallway. He contemplated tapping on TJ's door, but decided to wait, giving the boy a few more minutes of sleep. It had been a long, emotional week. Month actually.

And in a few hours, he was going to find out the fate of his family.

No matter what happened, things were going to be difficult for TJ. Toby understood that. He didn't look at this through rose-colored glasses. The social worker and the therapist had all told Toby that TJ could have lingering resentment toward his mother.

And toward Toby.

Maybe even Zinny.

Definitely toward Brooks, especially if Brooks never acknowledged being his father, which he'd yet to do.

Toby made his way into the kitchen and started a pot of coffee. That was the one thing that he didn't understand. If Serena really wanted to start over with Brooks and have TJ with them, why didn't Brooks stand up and shout from the rooftops he was TJ's father.

That's what Toby would be doing.

The machine made a few different gurgling noises

before spitting out the first few drops. The bitter smell ignited his senses as he continued to churn over all the same questions that he may never get answers to.

If they bothered him, he could only imagine what not knowing was doing to TJ. Or would do to him in the future. Toby had half a mind to call Brooks himself and ask what the hell his problem was, but that would be asking for trouble.

Toby filled two mugs with coffee and flavored creamer. He carried them up the stairs and to the master. "Here you go." He handed one to Zinny. "I better go wake the boy."

"Doesn't he have his own alarm clock?"

Toby laughed. "How many times did you oversleep when you were his age?"

"Not often," she said. "Have you met my mother? If I don't make it to the breakfast table in time, not only do I not get that meal, but she wouldn't give me lunch or money for lunch. And she'd make me walk to school, which meant I'd surely be late. No, thank you."

"Are you kidding me? Your dad gave you rides to school almost every day." Toby tapped her nose. "I heard he brought you hot lunch at least once a week."

"Where did you hear that?" Zinny slipped from the bed and raised up on her tiptoes, leaning into him, kissing his neck.

"Your mom," he admitted. "And everyone else at Sunday dinner. They all told me they weren't so lucky."

She shrugged. "The perks of being the baby."

He shook his head as he made his way down the corridor to TJ's room. He tapped on the door. "Come on, buddy. It's time to get up." He waited a few seconds.

Nothing.

"TJ. I'm coming in." He inched open the door. "What the hell?" He stormed inside the room. TJ's bed was empty. It was unmade, which meant he'd at least spent some of the night there, but who knew how long. His backpack, which he kept on his chair, was gone. Along with his tablet.

And his cell.

Fuck.

"What's wrong?" Zinny was at his side in seconds. "Shit. Where is he?"

"I don't know." Toby raced back to his bedroom. He yanked his phone from the charger and pulled up the *find my devices* application. "Goddammit. He turned the fucking thing off."

"I'm calling my dad, and then I'm calling the police," Zinny said.

Toby raked a hand across the top of his head. "Everything was fine. Where the fuck did he go and why? Maybe he left a note."

"You go look through his room. I'll go downstairs." Zinny squeezed his forearm. "We're going to find him."

"I just don't understand why he left." His eyes burned. His heart broke into a million pieces. Had he not read his own son right? Had TJ been playing him last night?

Nothing made sense.

"Teenagers are a tough breed. Especially middle schoolers. One minute they are playing board games and acting like a small child. The next minute they are swearing like drunken sailors, acting like idiots, thinking they are cool as shit."

"That's not making me feel any better, Zinny." He sucked in a deep breath and began searching his son's room for a clue as to where he went. He looked on the desk.

Lots of papers.

But no note as to where he might have gone.

He checked in the bed. Between the sheets. Under the mattress. Everywhere he could think of, but found nothing. He even went into the bathroom.

"Zinny? Did you find anything?" He jogged down the stairs, careful not to spill his coffee, though some sloshed out onto his hand. He found Zinny standing in the middle of the family room, pressing her cell to her ear. She waved a piece of paper over her head.

Toby snatched it from her hands.

"Daddy, I'm telling you, TJ left a strange note saying that he wanted to go for a run before he went to school. He hates running. I mean despises it. It's not the kind of workout he likes. Trust me, I know."

Toby scanned the note.

Hey, Dad,

I woke up early and decided to go for a run. Coach says I'm a little out of shape. Don't worry about me. I'll see you at the rink unless something at court happens.

TJ.

"Something's wrong." Toby snatched the phone. "Carter. He turned off his location services. He knows he's not supposed to do that. I can't track him. I have no idea when he left." Toby inhaled sharply. His chest stung as if he'd been stabbed. "He's never left the house before like this."

"Can you check his text messages or phone log on another device?" Carter asked.

"He took his tablet."

"Okay. Let's call the police. I'll call the judge. Then I'll have the family start looking. You two hang tight right there. I'll be over shortly."

"Thanks, Carter, but I can't sit here and do nothing," Toby said.

"You're going to do exactly that until I get there. And don't let Zinny leave. Hear me?"

"Yes, sir."

"Stop calling me that," Carter said. "See you in fifteen."

Toby tapped the red button and handed the phone back to Zinny. He sat down on the sofa and covered his face. "I'm going to say something that is mean, cruel, and I don't mean it, but I have to say it."

"If it has to do with me spending the night and thinking maybe if I hadn't, he'd still be here, trust me,

I've gone down that road a hundred times since we found out he was gone," Zinny said.

"That can't be the reason." Toby glanced up. "It was his idea, but I wonder if maybe I slept too hard because you were here or—"

"Toby. We can wonder this all day long. But it's not going to help us find him. And when we do, we'll have our answers and we'll deal with them."

He managed a weak smile. She was full of strength and right now, he relied on her more than he ever had before. She'd been his rock through so much.

"You're not why TJ left," Toby said. "You can't be because you're an angel. Something happened between the time we all went to bed and this morning. We should be calling Serena or going over to her house."

"I can't believe I'm going to be the voice of reason in this, but we need to let the police handle that one. We go over there, and one of us will most likely end up in handcuffs."

"Waiting sucks," Toby said. "When TJ does show his face, I'm going to have to ground him. Or something."

Zinny sat on the sofa and rested her arm on Toby's shoulders. "Something tells me about all you'll be able to do is hug him to death."

"Sounds about right."

Carter

. . .

Carter wrapped his arm around Zinny.

"I don't understand why we're here. I need to be out looking for my son." Toby paced the corridor of the courthouse. His mood had gone from concerned to worried sick ever since TJ hadn't shown up for school, which was understandable.

"Hanging out here isn't doing any good." Toby raked a hand across the top of his head. "It's been hours. He could be anywhere."

"I get it. Believe me. If I were you, I'd want to be racing all over town and wherever else I could think of. But the judge asked us—all of us, which includes Serena—to come here and wait for her." Carter rubbed the back of his neck. He had his entire family out there looking for TJ. Dax and Chablis were covering the areas near Candlewood Falls Prep. Merlot and Malbec headed to the west side of town and out, while Trey and Reisling took the east. The twins covered everywhere else while Weezer helped with Ashling and the newest member of the family.

The police were being helpful and since TJ hadn't indicated he planned on skipping school, they were now treating it as a missing person.

But that didn't make Carter feel better.

He'd read the note and while he didn't pretend to understand teenage boy lingo, in no way did he believe TJ ran away.

"Anyone notice who's not here?" Toby asked.

The fact that Serena wasn't anywhere to be seen, but her lawyer was, hadn't gone unnoticed by Carter.

"I just can't comprehend why he'd go with her." Toby took a seat on the bench in the corridor and cupped his face with both hands.

"We don't know that he did," Zinny said.

"Come on. Don't be so naive." Toby glared. "She must have texted him or called and gave him some compelling reason for him to sneak out. I just can't, for the life of me, figure out what that was."

The sound of high heels clicking on the tile floor caught Carter's attention. He turned, glancing over his shoulder.

The judge made her way down the corridor.

Before she made it halfway, Odette jumped out in front of her, but the judge pushed past, waving her hand.

That pretty much told Carter all he needed to know.

Serena wasn't in the building. She'd failed to report like the judge had asked everyone to, which could mean the worst.

She'd taken TJ and ran.

"You two stay right here," Carter demanded. He closed the gap between him and the judge. "Your Honor."

"Thank you for coming and bringing your client," the judge said. "How's he holding up?"

"Not well at all, Your Honor. As a matter of fact, I'm shocked I haven't had to tie him down."

The judge waved her arm toward the bend in the hallway. "I wanted to tell you in private that I spoke with Officer Bob who is here with TJ."

"Are you kidding me? Why aren't we telling Toby? Better yet, why isn't TJ being reunited with his father? Toby's out of his flipping mind."

"We will in a minute. But I needed TJ to spend a little time with the social worker first. And I wanted to inform you that Serena has been arrested."

"Jesus. For what?" Carter had a few guesses.

"For starters, she crossed state lines with TJ." The judge lifted a brow. "That boy is one smart kid. The moment they entered PA, he notified his social worker."

"Seriously?" Carter wanted to puff out his chest as though that were his grandson.

But he wasn't.

However, maybe someday that child would be part of his family. Now that he'd spent time with him and Toby, Carter wanted that to become a reality.

"He began texting the social worker, informing her what happened," she said, jerking her head. "Here come Officer Bob and TJ."

Carter glanced down the hallway and smiled.

Thank God.

Toby

Toby jumped to his feet. "TJ," he said as he raced down the hall, his arms stretched out wide. His heart thumped heavy in his chest. Tears welled in his eyes. For the first time during this entire ordeal, he'd actually been worried he might not see his son again. That Serena was actually going to disappear with him to some foreign country or something. "Are you okay? Are you hurt?"

"I'm fine, Dad." TJ collided with Toby and hugged him as if they hadn't seen each other in weeks. Months.

Toby closed his eyes and inhaled. Fourteen years of being a father filled his nostrils. His brain pulled up a million images.

TJ's first smile.

The first time he rolled over.

His first steps. The first time he skated all the way around the rink by himself and how proud he'd been. His first goal and the smile that brought to his face.

TJ's entire life flashed in Toby's mind.

"You scared the shit out of me." Toby squeezed harder. "I don't know what I'd do if anything ever happened to you."

"I'm so sorry I worried you. But I didn't know what else to do when Mom called me."

Toby cupped his son's face. "Oh, we're going to talk

about that later. You always have choices and you should have told me right away."

"I don't mean to ruin a perfectly good reunion, but I need to speak with all of you." The judge appeared.

"Am I in trouble?" TJ asked.

"No, son. Not by me. But your father is right. You could have handled this a different way." The judge reached out and rested her hand on TJ's shoulder. "Let's go into my office, okay?"

TJ nodded.

"I'll wait out here for you," Zinny said.

Toby had been brutal with his attitude toward Zinny and he owed her a million and one apologies. "Thanks." He smiled.

"Can she come with us, Your Honor?" TJ asked. "I know she's not officially family yet, but I think that's only a matter of time."

"If it's that important to you, Zinny is welcome." The judge looped her arm around TJ. "And if it's okay with your dad."

"Dad? Can she come too?" TJ's eyes were swollen and bloodshot.

"Of course." Toby had never seen his boy so distraught before. He followed the judge and Carter into the judge's chambers.

He took a seat at the far end of the conference table. TJ sat to his right, and Zinny was to his left. Carter sat close to Zinny.

Growing up, Toby hadn't felt close to his parents.

As a matter of fact, he'd felt disconnected. His father put way too much pressure on him, and his mom hadn't ever stood up for him. It wasn't until after his dad passed that he realized how controlling his father had been over his mom and how unhappy she'd been.

It broke his heart to know how truly bad his parents' marriage had been and he hadn't done much better for himself.

He glanced toward Zinny and took her hand. If he had any doubts about wanting to start a life with her, they'd all washed away in this moment. Most women would have left long ago.

But not Zinny.

She stuck by his side during his darkest hour. When he needed an angel to guide him through, she was there, giving him a loving smile. Her love was unconditional and she deserved for him to be a better man.

"TJ," the judge said. "You and I are the only ones in this room who know what happened. Would you like to fill in your dad, or shall I start?"

"I know my dad, and he'd want for me to take responsibility for what I did and tell my story." TJ shifted, turning to face Toby. "First, I do want to say I'm sorry for worrying you and everyone else. But when you hear what Mom was planning, you'll understand."

Toby took in a slow breath. "I'm listening."

"Mom has been messaging me all along," TJ started. "At first, I didn't tell you when she reached out because I wanted to talk to and see my mom. I missed her."

That statement damn near brought Toby to his knees. It killed him that his boy had to live with this legacy.

Add Brooks into the mix and Toby worried what kind of effect this would have on TJ's heart.

Toby knew how his father had hardened his.

"Our conversations were about school and hockey and just normal stuff, but every once in a while, she'd toss in how she had this big plan for our future. When the custody proceeding started, she told me she knew the courts were going to give her custody and that Brooks was to claim me and my adoption was going to be voided."

Toby swallowed his rage. He squeezed Zinny's hand so hard she had to wiggle it to remind him to stop. "I'm so sorry she said those things to you and scared you into thinking that could happen. I'm your father. You're my son. No one can take that from us."

"I actually told Mom that, but she said the courts can. And she emailed me past cases that proved it two days ago. She told me as soon as Brooks filed whatever paperwork, that was going to be it, and last night, Mom texted me telling me that Brooks made a declaration to the court for paternity and that it was going to be granted. That happened right as we were all going to bed. I thought that was crazy because who at the courthouse works past five. Mom then asked me to meet her for breakfast so we could make plans. Because some of what she said didn't make sense, I thought it might be a good idea to meet her."

"Without telling me?" Toby tried not to show too much anger.

"I thought if I could find out what her plans were, I could take it to the judge. I didn't think she was going to kidnap me," TJ said with thick emotion. He glanced down at his hands in his lap.

"Kidnapped?" Toby blinked. "You didn't go with her willingly?"

TJ shook his head. "When I told her I wouldn't leave, she told me if I didn't, she'd hurt Zinny."

"Hurt how?" Carter asked.

"I don't want to say." TJ slumped in his chair and swiped his cheeks.

Toby wrapped his arm around his son. "It's okay. This is a safe space."

TJ shook his head.

"I think we can give him a pass on this one. Since I know the story, I'll fill in the blanks here," the judge said. "Serena told TJ she had distasteful pictures of Zinny and she would use them to destroy her."

Zinny pressed her hands on the table. "Does she have them? Because if she does, she could still use them and—"

"I issued a search warrant. If they exist, we'll make sure they don't see the light of day," the judge said.

"Thank you." Zinny blew out a puff of air. She glanced at Toby. "How did she get those pictures?"

"It's my fault," TJ said. "She asked me for Dad's passwords a while ago, before I understood what was going on. I'm sorry."

"Oh. That's not your fault," Zinny said with conviction. "And don't ever think it is. Not that this is my place, but the only thing you did wrong was sneaking out without telling your dad you were leaving. Other than that, none of this is your fault."

"But if I hadn't given her those passwords—"

"You didn't know," Zinny said. "I don't want you thinking twice about that. Okay?"

TJ nodded.

Toby choked on his breath. He'd hit the jackpot with Zinny. Not many women would be so understanding.

"Okay, TJ. So, you got in the car with her out of fear," the judge said.

"She looked at her phone and told me that the courts had decided and that my dad wasn't my dad anymore and that Brooks was waiting for us in Ohio."

"I'm so sorry, TJ," Toby said.

"TJ," the judge started. "You were smart to contact your social worker once you crossed over state lines."

"I saw that on some television show but wasn't sure if it was true or not," TJ said.

"Oh, it's true," the judge said. "I'm sorry you had to see your mother get arrested."

"Does this mean she's going to prison?" TJ asked with tears running down his cheeks.

He still loved her and Toby could understand that. He never stopped loving his dad even though on his deathbed his father told him what a shit son he'd been.

But Toby had to protect his son. He would help him through this time in his life so he didn't have too many deep emotional scars, and even though he didn't have a mom who could love him unconditionally, TJ did have a lot of people in his life who did.

Toby would make sure of it.

"Because this is now her second offense, it's probable," the judge said. "But I can't honestly say one way or the other. The way the judicial system works is tricky and I won't be presiding over that case."

"And what about Brooks?" TJ asked. "Is it true what my social worker told me when I first got here?"

"You saw the social worker? Before me?" Toby asked. "Why didn't I know this?"

"Toby," Carter said. "A lot has happened this morning and everyone just wanted to make sure that TJ was okay. Part of that was a conversation with her."

While Toby understood that on some levels, he was TJ's father. He should have been the first one who got to see his boy.

"Can someone please tell me if what the social worker said is true?" TJ pleaded.

"I don't know what she said." Toby had never felt so hopeless in his life.

"I'm the only one in this room who knows that answer." The judge leaned forward, holding a tablet in her hands. "I had Mr. Halsteder brought into my chambers this morning."

Toby rolled his neck. That name made his fingers twitch. All he could think about was making a fist. He truly loathed Brooks. He didn't understand how anyone could be so cruel to a child.

"Mr. Halsteder had nothing to do with the attempted kidnapping. His only role had been when Serena outed him as TJ's biological father. He informed me, and I let the social worker know, he has no intention of interfering with TJ and Toby's relationship. That he gave up his parental rights and he intends to honor that agreement."

"So. It's true? I don't have to worry he's going to try to take me away from my dad?" TJ asked with a shaky voice.

"No, son. You don't have to worry about that at all," the judge said. "And even though I have to give an official statement in court, I think it's okay to say this here, but considering what has transpired, I will be granting full custody to your dad."

"Really?" TJ sat up taller.

"Yes," the judge said.

"That's awesome." TJ smiled. "Can we go home now?"

"Not just yet." The judge stood and glanced at her watch. "Court will reconvene in fifteen minutes. I believe we can wrap everything up within the hour.

Your dad will be free to go after that. I suggest he let you play hooky for the rest of the day."

"At least until hockey practice," TJ said. "I can't miss that."

The judge laughed. "I'm a big Dax Fabion fan. I'm going to have to come watch one of your games next year."

"He's an excellent coach," TJ said. "Best I've ever had."

"Even I have to agree with that." Toby laughed.

The judge waved her hand toward the door. "I'll see you all in court in a few minutes."

Toby followed his son out the door. Carter and Zinny were two steps behind him. Once in the hallway, he turned and pulled his son in for a big hug. "I love you, TJ. I can't tell you how scared I was this morning, not knowing where you were."

"I'm really sorry," TJ said softly.

Toby took a step back. "I understand why you did it, but let's not ever do that again, okay?"

TJ nodded.

"Before we go into court, I need to speak with Zinny for a minute," Toby said. "Carter, do you mind hanging out with TJ for a second?"

"Not at all." Carter nodded.

"Thanks." Toby took Zinny by the hand.

"Why do I all of a sudden have a weird feeling in my gut?" Zinny tucked a few strands of hair behind her ear.

He took her into his arms and gently kissed her lips. "Does it feel like butterflies?"

"You're being weird and my dad and TJ are staring at us."

Toby wasn't happy that his ex-wife was going to jail, but he was thrilled that he could close the book on this part of his life and open a new adventure. One where he could bask in the love he hadn't expected he'd ever find. Not that he'd gone looking for it.

"Let everyone stare," he said. "Zinfandel. You're my sweet angel and I can't believe how lucky I am to be the man who loves you."

Sunday Dinner
One Month Later

"I was having fun playing," Zinny stared at Chablis.

"I need a break." Chablis tugged her arm.

Zinny sat on the tree stump in the backyard between the house and the vineyards. Behind her, Toby and TJ played flag football with the rest of her family. It was a family tradition and Zinny preferred to be in the thick of the game, where Chablis almost always sat on the sidelines.

"Why are we sitting here and not on the porch with Mom, Toby's mom, and Eliza Jane?"

"I just wanted a moment with my baby sister,"

Chablis said. "TJ is really thriving. Dax said he's becoming quite the little leader on the hockey team."

Zinny had no idea what had gotten into Chablis, but she would enjoy a private conversation. "His grades are improving, and his entire demeanor is different. I can't believe I'm going to say this, but I do hate that his mom had to go to prison for this to happen."

"Dax said she still reaches out to him," Chablis said.

"She calls sometimes, but we have a deal that he doesn't speak to her without Toby sitting next to him. He doesn't open emails either. So far, he's adhering to those rules, and he's only talked to her three times. Not much has changed with her. TJ's also seeing a therapist once a week. Toby goes with him every other week. It's really helping."

"It shows." Chablis nodded. "How are you doing? How are things with you and Toby?"

"Good." Zinny couldn't complain about how the relationship had progressed. "I still have to deal with funny looks from people sometimes in town and every once in a while, someone says something stupid to Toby about cradle-robbing, but otherwise, things are great. I really love him."

"We can all tell. And he loves you too."

"I know he does." Zinny sighed. Her parents had always told her that patience was a virtue. But that wasn't her strong suit. Far from it. She'd always been the kind of kid that once she made a decision, she didn't like waiting, and she'd decided she wanted a life and a family with Toby.

He was divorced and Serena was out of his life.

They loved each other.

So why wait to get married? Or even have kids? She didn't care that she was young. She knew she wanted a child with Toby.

"How's married life?" Zinny asked, needing to move the topic off her and Toby. Her sister had been married for two full weeks, but she and Dax had been trying to have a baby for at least two months. "Are you pregnant yet?"

Chablis' cheeks turned bright red.

"Oh, my God. You are."

"We just found out, so you can't tell anyone yet. Especially Mom and Dad."

"Why don't you say something today? Come on, that's what Sunday dinners are for," Zinny said.

Chablis laughed. "I know. But there is only so much excitement this family can take in one day and someone else has something they want to announce."

"Who?" Zinny leaned forward. "It's too early for Eliza Jane to be pregnant again, though I know they want to have two right away and be done with it."

"I'm not going to ruin the surprise."

"Oh. Are Mom and Dad getting remarried? That's it, isn't it?" Zinny rubbed her hands together.

"No. That's not it," a male voice said from behind her. "But someone does want to ask someone to marry them."

Her heart beat so fast and furious she felt it in her throat.

Slowly, she turned. Her entire family stood behind Toby, who was on bended knee, holding out a ring. She glanced over her shoulder. "Everyone already knows you're pregnant, don't they?"

Chablis nodded. "We just needed a way to get your back to the game so we could set this up."

Zinny waved her finger at Chablis. "You're sneaky."

"And you're leaving me hanging here like a fool," Toby said. "Would you mind giving me your attention?"

"Oh. Sorry." Zinny faced Toby. "Did you want to ask me something?"

Her father burst out laughing.

Toby closed his eyes for a moment. "Zinny. I love you. TJ loves you."

"He's right. I do." TJ tossed the football from one hand to the other. "But can we get on with this? My team is down by seven points, and Weezer says we only have half an hour before dinner's ready."

"I knew I should have taken you out—alone—for a romantic dinner."

Zinny cupped his face. "No. I wouldn't have this any other way." She lowered her gaze and gasped. The ring was an emerald.

Her favorite.

And it was huge.

Tears welled in her eyes.

"I love you, Zinny. Will you do me the honor and be my wife?"

"Oh, hell yes." She held out her hand.

He placed the ring on her finger. It fit perfectly.

She wrapped her arms around him, and they tumbled backward onto the ground. Her lips found his and she kissed him. Hard.

"Ew. Gross. Get a room," TJ said.

"Agreed," her father echoed. "Come on. Maybe Weezer will fill in for your dad. She's actually really good."

"Thank you," Zinny whispered.

"For what?" Toby helped her to her feet. He pulled a few twigs out of her hair.

"Doing this with my family. It means a lot to them."

"And to you."

She nodded.

"Family is everything." He ran his thumb over her lower lip. "You and TJ are the most important people in my world. I'd do anything for you, including sharing these moments with the rest of our family."

"You said our family." If she hadn't been in love with him already, she would have fallen for him in that moment.

"Everyone here has treated me and TJ as though we are blood. It's what I've tried to show TJ his entire life. That families aren't always about who and what you are born into, but what you make. We're lucky that I was kissed by the lips of an angel."

Thank you for taking the time to read *Lips Of An Angel.* Please feel free to leave an honest review. Next in the series is: *Kisses Sweeter than Wine,* followed by: *A Little Bit Whiskey.*

Also by K.M. Fawcett is WILD IN LOVE: Can a bad boy and a good girl overcome their fears to find true love?

And in WILDE TREASURES: While searching for a hidden fortune, can two lonely adventurers discover some treasurers are more precious than gold.

ACKNOWLEDGMENTS

A big thank you to Stacey Wilk and K.M. Fawcett for inviting me into Candlewood Falls.

ABOUT THE AUTHOR

Jen Talty is the *USA Today* Bestselling Author of Contemporary Romance, Romantic Suspense, and Paranormal Romance. In the fall of 2020, her short story was selected and featured in a 1001 Dark Nights Anthology.

Regardless of the genre, her goal is to take you on a ride that will leave you floating under the sun with warmth in your heart. She writes stories about broken heroes and heroines who aren't necessarily looking for romance, but in the end, they find the kind of love books are written about :).

She first started writing while carting her kids to one hockey rink after the other, averaging 170 games per year between 3 kids in 2 countries and 5 states. Her first book, IN TWO WEEKS was originally published in 2007. In 2010 she helped form a publishing company (Cool Gus Publishing) with *NY Times* Bestselling Author Bob Mayer where she ran the technical side of the business through 2016.

Jen is currently enjoying the next phase of her life...the empty nester! She and her husband reside in Jupiter, Florida.

Grab a glass of vino, kick back, relax, and let the romance roll in...

Sign up for my *Newsletter (https://dl.bookfunnel.com/82gm8b9k4y)* where I often give away free books before publication.

Join my private Facebook group (https://www.facebook.com/groups/191706547909047/) where I post exclusive excerpts and discuss all things murder and love!

Never miss a new release. Follow me on Amazon:amazon.com/author/jentalty

And on Bookbub: bookbub.com/authors/jen-talty

ALSO BY JEN TALTY

Everyone needs a SAFE HARBOR!

Mine To Keep

Mine To Save

Mine To Protect

Mine to Hold

Mine to Love

Check out LOVE IN THE ADIRONDACKS!

Shattered Dreams

An Inconvenient Flame

The Wedding Driver

Clear Blue Sky

Blue Moon

Before the Storm

NY STATE TROOPER SERIES (also set in the Adirondacks!)

In Two Weeks

Dark Water

Deadly Secrets

Murder in Paradise Bay

To Protect His own

Deadly Seduction

When A Stranger Calls

His Deadly Past

The Corkscrew Killer

First Responders: A spin-off from the NY State Troopers series

Playing With Fire

Private Conversation

The Right Groom

After The Fire

Caught In The Flames

Chasing The Fire

Legacy Series

Dark Legacy

Legacy of Lies

Secret Legacy

Emerald City

Investigate Away

Sail Away

Fly Away

Flirt Away

Hawaii Brotherhood Protectors

Waylen Unleashed

Bowie's Battle

Colorado Brotherhood Protectors

Fighting For Esme

Defending Raven

Fay's Six

Darius' Promise

Yellowstone Brotherhood Protectors

Guarding Payton

Wyatt's Mission

Corbin's Mission

Candlewood Falls

Rivers Edge

The Buried Secret

Its In His Kiss

Lips Of An Angel

Kisses Sweeter than Wine

A Little Bit Whiskey

It's all in the Whiskey

Johnnie Walker

Georgia Moon

Jack Daniels

Jim Beam

Whiskey Sour

Whiskey Cobbler

Whiskey Smash

Irish Whiskey

The Monroes

Color Me Yours

Color Me Smart

Color Me Free

Color Me Lucky

Color Me Ice

Color Me Home

Search and Rescue

Protecting Ainsley

Protecting Clover

Protecting Olympia

Protecting Freedom

Protecting Princess

Protecting Marlowe

Fallport Rescue Operations

Searching for Madison

Searching for Haven

Searching for Pandora

Searching for Stormi

Talon's Honor

Arthur's Honor

Rex's Honor

Kent's Honor

Buddy's Honor

Aegis Network Short Stories

Max & Milian

A Christmas Miracle

Spinning Wheels

Holiday's Vacation

The Brotherhood Protectors

Out of the Wild

Rough Justice

Rough Around The Edges

Rough Ride

Rough Edge

Rough Beauty

The Brotherhood Protectors

The Saving Series

Saving Love

Saving Magnolia

Saving Leather

Hot Hunks

Cove's Blind Date Blows Up

My Everyday Hero – Ledger

Tempting Tavor

Malachi's Mystic Assignment

Needing Neor

Holiday Romances

A Christmas Getaway

Alaskan Christmas

Whispers

Christmas In The Sand

Heroes & Heroines on the Field

Taking A Risk

Tee Time

A New Dawn

The Blind Date

Spring Fling

Summers Gone

Winter Wedding

The Awakening

Fated Moons

The Collective Order

The Lost Sister

The Lost Soldier

The Lost Soul

The Lost Connection

The New Order